THE SECRET WAR

Harris stared at the photo a long while. This girl? A spy? How improbable that seemed! But his superiors could not be mistaken. And it was Harris' job to kill her, now—a task he had no option of refusing. He was Darruui—a Servant of the Spirit. He could not betray his trust. . . . He paused a moment outside her door, then nudged the door signal.

"Who is it?"

"It's me. Abner. I have to see you, Beth."

"It's late. It's the middle of the night."

"I'm sorry if I woke you. It's important that I talk to you."

"Hold on," came the sleepy reply from inside. "Let me get something on, Abner."

He waited. A moment passed, then the door slid silently open. Beth smiled at him warmly. She had donned a flimsy gown that concealed her body as if she were wearing so much gauze. A strange swirl of emotions rushed through him. Was his Earthman's outward form betraying him?

But Harris was far more interested in the tiny, glittering object she held firmly in her hand, trained on his skull.

It was a Medlin disruptor-pistol. . . .

THE SILENT INVADERS

ROBERT SILVERBERG
THE SILENT INVADERS

A TOM DOHERTY ASSOCIATES BOOK

THE SILENT INVADERS Copyright © 1963 by Ace Books, Inc.
VALLEY BEYOND TIME Copyright © 1957, 1985 by Robert Silverberg

A TOR Book

Published by Tom Doherty Associates
49 West 24 Street
New York, N.Y. 10010

Cover art by Tom Kidd

First TOR printing: October 1985

ISBN: 0-812-55460-4
CAN. ED.: 0-812-55461-2

Printed in the United States of America

This book is for
RADAMES

The
Silent
Invaders

One

The prime-class starship *Lucky Lady* came thundering out of overdrive half a million miles from Earth, and phased into the long, steady ion-drive glide at Earth-norm gravitation toward the orbiting depot. In his second-class cabin aboard the starship, the man whose papers said he was Major Abner Harris of the Inter-stellar Development Corps stared anxiously, critically, at his face in the mirror. He was checking, for what must have been the hundredth time, to make sure that there was no sign of where his tendrils once had been.

There was, of course, no sign. He looked the very image of an Earthman.

He smiled; and the even-featured, undistinguished face the medics had put on him drew back, lips rising

3

obediently in the corners, cheeks tightening, neat white teeth momentarily on display. It was a good smile; an Earthman's smile down to the last degree.

Major Harris scowled, and the face darkened as a scowling face should darken.

The face behaved well. The synthetic white skin acted as if it were his own. The surgeons back on Darruu had done their usual superb job on him. His appearance was a triumph of the art.

They had removed the fleshy four-inch-long tendrils that sprouted at every Darruui's temples; they had covered his deep golden-hued skin with an overlay of convincingly Terran white, and grafted it so skillfully that by now it had become his real skin.

Contact lenses had turned his eyes from their normal red to a Terran blue-gray. Hormone treatments had caused hair to sprout on head and body, thick Earthman hair where none had been before. The surgeons had not meddled with his internal plumbing, because that was too great a task even for their skill. Inwardly he remained alien, with the efficient Darruui digestive organ where a Terran had so many incredible feet of intestine, and with the double heart and the sturdy liver just back of his three lungs.

Inside he was alien. Behind the walls of his skull, he was Aar Khiilom of the city of Helasz—a Darruui of the highest class, a Servant of the Spirit. But he had to forget his Darruui identity now, he had to cloak himself in the Earthman identity he wore. He was not Aar Khiilom, he told himself doggedly, but Major Abner Harris.

He knew Major Harris' biography in the greatest deta'!, and reviewed it constantly, so that it lay beneath the conscious part of his mind like the hidden nine-tenths of an iceberg, ready to come automatically to use when needed in an emergency.

Major Abner Harris, according to the identity they had created for him, had been born in 2520, in Cincinnati, Ohio. (*Cincinnati's a city,* he thought. *Ohio is a state. Remember that and don't mix them up!*) Ohio was one of the United States of America, which was a large political sub-unit of the planet Earth.

Major Abner Harris was now aged 42—with a good hundred years of his lifespan left. He had attended Western Reserve University, studying galactography; graduated '43. Entered the Interstellar Redevelopment Corps '46, commissioned '50, now holding the rank of Major. Successful diplomatic-military missions to Altair VII, Sirius IX, Procyon II, Alpheratz IV, and Sirius VII.

Major Harris was unmarried. His parents had been killed in a highway jet-crash in '44. He had no known living relatives with a greater consanguinity than D+. Height five feet ten, weight 220, color fair, retinal index point 033.

Major Harris was visiting Earth on vacation. He was to spend eight months relaxing on his native world before reassignment to his next planetary post.

Eight months, thought the alien being who called himself Major Abner Harris, would certainly be ample time for Major Abner Harris to lose himself in

the swarming billions of Earth and carry out the
purposes for which he had been sent.

The *Lucky Lady* was on the last lap of her journey
across half a million light-years, bearing passengers
to Earth and points along the route. Harris had boarded
the starship on Alpheratz IV, after having been shipped
there from Darruu via private warpship. For the past
three weeks, while the giant vessel had slipped gently
through the sleek gray tunnel in the continuum that
was its overdrive channel, Major Harris had been
practicing how to walk at Earth-norm gravity.

Darruu was a large world—its radius was 11,000
miles—and though its density was not as great as
Earth's, still the gravitational attraction was half again
as intense. Harris had been born and raised under
Darruu's gravity of 1.5 Earth-norm. Or, as Harris
had thought of it in the days when his mind centered
not on Earth but on Darruu, Earth's gravity was .67
Darruu-norm.

Either way, it meant that his muscles would be
functioning in a gravitational field two-thirds as strong
as the one they had developed in. For a while, at
least, he would have a tendency to lift his feet too
high, to overstep, to exaggerate every motion. If anyone noticed, he could use the excuse that he had
spent most of his time in service on heavy planets,
and that would explain away some of his awkwardness.

Some of it, but not all. A native-born Earther, no
matter how many years he spends on heavy worlds,
still never forgets how to cope with Earth-norm grav-

ity. Harris had to learn that from scratch. He *did* learn it, painstakingly, during the three weeks of overdrive travel across the universe toward the system of Sol.

Now the journey was almost over. All that remained was the transfer from the starship to an Earth shuttle, and then he could begin his life as an Earthman.

Earth hung outside the main viewport twenty feet from Harris' cabin. He stared at it. He saw a great green ball of a world, with two huge continents sprawling here, another land-mass there. A giant moon was moving in slow procession around the planet, keeping one pockmarked face eternally staring inward, the other glaring at outer space like a single beady dark eye.

The sight made Harris homesick.

Darruu was nothing like this. Darruu, viewed from space, had the appearance of a giant red fruit, covered over by the crimson mist that was the upper layer of its atmosphere. Beneath that, an observer could discern the great blue seas and the two hemisphere-large continents of Darraa and Darroo.

And the moons, Harris thought nostalgically. Seven glistening blank faces ranged like gleaming coins in the sky, each at its own angle to the ecliptic, each taking its place in the sky nightly like a gem moved by subtle clockwork. And the mating of the moons, when the seven came together once a year to form a fiercely radiant diadem that filled half the sky . . .

Angrily he cut the train of thought.

You're an Earthman, remember? You can't afford the luxury of nostalgia. Forget Darruu.

A voice on a speaker overhead said, "Please return to your cabins, ladies and gentlemen. In approximately eleven minutes we will come to a rest at the main spaceborne depot. Those passengers who are intending to transfer here will please notify their area steward."

Harris returned to his cabin while the voice methodically repeated the statement in several of the other languages of Earth. Earth still spoke more than a dozen major tongues, which he was surprised to learn; Darruu had reached linguistic homogeneity some three thousand years or more in the past, and it was odd to think that so highly developed a planet as Earth still had many languages.

Minutes ticked by. The public address system hummed again, finally, and at last came the word that the *Lucky Lady* had ended its ion-drive cruise and was tethered to the orbital satellite. It was time for him to leave the ship.

Harris left his cabin for the last time and headed down-ramp to the designated room on D Deck where outgoing passengers were assembling. He recognized a few faces of people he had spoken to briefly on his trip, and he nodded to them, stiffly, with the dignity of a military man.

A clerk came up to him. "Is everything all right, sir? Are there any questions?"

"Where is the baggage?" Harris asked.

"Your baggage will be shipped across automatically. You don't have to worry about that."

"I wouldn't want to lose it."

"Everything's tagged, sir. The scanners never miss. There's nothing to worry about."

Harris nodded. His baggage was important.

"Anything else, sir?"

"No. That will be all."

More than three hundred of the *Lucky Lady*'s many passengers were leaving ship here. Harris found himself being herded along with the others through an arising airlock. Several dozen ungainly little ferries hovered just outside, linked to the huge starliner by swaying, precariously flimsy connecting tubes.

Harris entered one of the tubes, clinging to the guard rail as he crossed over, and found a seat on the ferry. The ferry filled rapidly, and with a spurt of ionic energy whisked itself across the emptiness of the void in a flight only a few minutes long. In another moment, Harris was once again crossing tubes, as the ferry unloaded its passengers into the main airlock of Orbiting Station Number One.

Bright lights greeted him. His remodeled eyes adjusted easily to the blaze. Another loudspeaker boomed, "*Lucky Lady* passengers who are continuing on to Earth report immediately to Routing Channel Four. Repeat: *Lucky Lady* passengers continuing on to Earth report immediately to Routing Channel Four. Passengers transshipping to other starlines should go to the nearest routing desk at once. Repeat: Passengers transshipping to other starlines . . ."

Harris began to feel like an article of merchandise. There was something damnedly impersonal about the way these Earthers kept shunting you from pillar to post. On Darruu, there was a good deal more ceremony involved.

But this, as he had to keep in mind, was not Darruu.

He followed a winking green light through a maze of passageways and found himself at a place that proclaimed itself, in an infinity of languages, to be Routing Channel Four. He joined the line.

It took half an hour for him to reach the front. A bland-faced Earther behind the desk smiled at him and said, "Your papers, please?"

Harris handed over the little fabrikoid portfolio. The spaceport official riffled sleepily through it and handed it back without a word, stamping a symbol on the margin of one page. A nod of the head sent Harris onward through the doorway.

As he boarded the Earth-Orbiter shuttle, an attractive stewardess gave him a warm smile. "Welcome aboard, Major. Has it been a good trip so far?"

"No complaints, thanks."

"I'm glad. Here's some information you might like to look over."

He took the multigraphed sheet of paper from her and lowered himself into a seat. The sheet contained information of the sort a tourist was likely to want to know. Harris scanned it quickly.

"The Orbiting Station is located eighty thousand

miles from Earth. It is locked in a perpetual twenty-four hour orbit that keeps it hovering approximately above Quito, Ecuador, South America. During a year the Orbiting Station serves an average of 8,500,000 travellers—"

Harris finished reading the sheet, crumpled it, and stuffed it into the disposal in his armrest. As a mental exercise he visualized South America and tried to locate Ecuador. When he had done that to his own satisfaction, he leaned back, and eyed his fellow passengers aboard the Earthbound shuttle. There were about fifty of them.

For all he knew, five were disguised Darruui like himself. He would have no sure way of telling. Or they might be enemies—Medlins—likewise in disguise. Or, he thought, possibly he was surrounded by agents of Earth's own intelligence corps, who had already penetrated his disguise and who would sweep him efficiently and smoothly into custody the moment the shuttle touched down on the surface of Earth.

Trouble lay on every hand. Inwardly Major Harris felt calm, sure of his abilities, sure of his purpose, though there was the faint twinge of homesickness for Darruu that he knew he would never be entirely able to erase from his mind.

The shuttle banked into a steep deceleration curve. The artificial gravitation aboard the ship remained constant, of course.

Earth drew near.

Landing came.

The shuttle hung poised over the skin of the landing field for thirty seconds, then dropped, touching down easily. A gantry crane shuffled out to support the ship, and buttress-legs sprang outward from the sides of the hull.

A steward's voice said unctuously, "Passengers will please assemble at the airlock in single file."

The passengers duly assembled, and duly marched out through the airlock, out into the atmosphere of Earth. A green omnibus waited outside on the field to take them to the arrivals building. The fifty passengers obediently filed into the omnibus.

Harris found a seat by the window and stared out across the broad field. A yellow sun was in the blue sky. The air was cold and thin; he shivered involuntarily, and drew his cloak around him for warmth.

"Cold?"

The man who had asked the question shared Harris' seat with him—a fat, deeply tanned, prosperous man with thick lips and a look of deep concern on his face.

"A bit," Harris said.

"That's odd. Nice balmy spring day like this, you'd think everybody would be enjoying the weather. You pick up malaria in the Service, or something?"

Harris grinned and shook his head. "No, nothing like that. But I've been on some pretty hot worlds the last ten years. Anything under ninety degrees or so and I start shivering. Force of habit."

The other chuckled and said, "Must be near eighty in the shade today."

"I'll be accustomed to Earth weather again before long," Harris said easily. "You know how it is. Once an Earthman, always an Earthman."

"Yeah. What planets you been to?"

"Classified," Harris said.

"Oh. Oh, yeah. I suppose you have to."

His seatmate abruptly lost interest in him. Harris made a mental note to carry out a trifling adjustment on his body thermostat, first decent chance he got. His skin was lined with subminiaturized heating and refrigerating units—just one of the many useful modifications the surgeons had given him.

Darruu's mean temperature was 120 degrees, on the scale used by the Earthers in his allegedly native land. (What kind of civilization could it be, Harris wondered, that had three or four different scales for measuring temperature?) When the temperature on Darruu dropped to 80, Darruui cursed the cold and bundled into winter clothes. The temperature was 80 now, and he was uncomfortably cold, in sharp and revealing contrast to everyone about him. He told himself that he would simply have to go on freezing for most of the day, at least, until in a moment of privacy he could make the necessary adjustments. Around him, the Earthers seemed to be perspiring and feeling discomfort because of the heat.

The bus filled finally, and spurted across the field for a ten-minute trip to a high-domed building of gleaming metal and green plastic. The driver called out, "First stop is customs. Have your papers ready."

Inside, Harris found his baggage already waiting for him at a counter labelled HAM-HAT. There were two suitcases, both of them equipped with topological secret compartments that no one was likely to detect.

He surrendered his passport. The customs man glanced at it, then riffled it in front of an optical scanner that made an instant copy of its contents.

"Open the suitcases."

Harris pressed his thumb to the opener-plate. The suitcases sprang open. The customs man poked through them perfunctorily, nodded, pushed a button that activated an electronic spybeam, and waited for a telltale buzz. Nothing buzzed.

"Anything to declare?"

"Nothing."

"Okay. You're clear. Close 'em up."

Harris locked the suitcases again, and the customs official briefly touched a tracer-stamp to them. It left no visible imprint, but the photonic scanners at every door would be watching for the radiations, and no one with an unstamped item of luggage could get through the electronic barriers.

"Where do I go now?" Harris asked.

"Your next stop's Immigration, Major."

At Immigration they studied his passport briefly, noted that he was a government employee, and passed him along to Health. Here he felt a moment of alarm; about one out of every fifty incoming passengers from a starship was detained at random, to be given a comprehensive medical exam by way of plague-watch. If the finger fell upon him, he knew, the game was up right here and now. Ten seconds in front of a fluoroscope would tell them that nobody with that kind of skeletal structure had ever been born in Cincinnati, Ohio.

The finger fell elsewhere. He got through Health with nothing more than a rudimentary checkup. At the last desk his passport was stamped with a reentry visa, and the clerk said, "You haven't been on Earth for a long time, have you, Major?"

"Not in ten years. Hope things haven't changed too much."

"The women are still the same, anyway," the clerk said with what was meant to be a sly leer. He shuffled Harris' papers together, stuck them back in the portfolio, and handed them to him. "Everything's in order, Major. Go straight ahead and out the door to your left. And lots of luck on Earth."

Harris thanked him and moved along, gripping one suitcase in each hand. A month ago, at the beginning of his journey, the suitcases had seemed heavy to him. But that had been back on Darruu; here on Earth they weighed only two-thirds as much. He carried them jauntily.

Soon it will be spring on Darruu, he thought. The red-leaved jasaar trees would blossom and their sweet perfume would fill the air.

With an angry inner scowl he blanked out the thought. Such needless self-torment was stupid. He was no Darruui. He was Major Abner Harris, late of Cincinnati, here on Earth for eight months of vacation.

He knew his orders. He was to establish residence, avoid detection, and in the second week of his stay make contact with the chief Darruui agent on Earth. Further instructions would come from him.

Two

It took twenty minutes by helitaxi to reach the metropolitan area from the spaceport. Blithely handling the Terran currency as though he had been using it all his life, Harris paid the driver, tipped him precisely fifteen percent, and got out. He had asked for and he had been taken to a hotel in the heart of the city—the Spaceways Hotel. There was one of them in every major spaceport city in the galaxy; the spacelines operated the chain under a jointly-owned corporation for the benefit of travellers who had no place to stay on the planet of their destination.

He signed in and was given a room on the 58th floor. The Earther on duty at the desk checked out his papers and, as he handed Harris the registry plaque, said, "You don't mind heights, do you, Major?"

"Not at all."

A boy scooped up his bags. On Darruu, it would be a humiliation to carry another person's bags. But this was not Darruu, Harris reminded himself once again, and when he reached his room he gave the boy who had carried his bags a demi-unit piece, received grateful thanks, and was left in solitude.

He locked the door. For the first time since leaving Darruu he was really *alone*. Thumbing open his suitcases, he dextrously performed the series of complex stress-pressures that gave access to the hidden areas of the grips; miraculously, the suitcases expanded to nearly twice their former volume as he unsealed them. There was nothing like packing your belongings in a tesseract if you really wanted to keep the customs men away from your property.

Busily, he unpacked.

The first thing to emerge was a small device which fit neatly and virtually invisibly to the inside of the room door. It was a jammer for spybeams. It insured a good measure of privacy.

A disruptor-pistol came next. Harris slipped it into his tunic-pocket after checking the charge.

Several books; a flask of Darruui wine; a photograph of his birth-tree. Bringing these things had not increased the risk he ran, since if any of them had been discovered it would only have been after much more seriously incriminating information had come to light.

The subspace communicator, for example. Or the narrow-beam amplifier he would use in making known

his presence here to the other members of the secret
Darruui cadre established on Earth.

Harris finished unpacking, restored his suitcases to
their three-dimensional state, and took a tiny scalpel
from the toolkit he had unpacked. Quickly stripping
off his trousers, he laid bare the desensitized area in
the fleshy part of his thigh, stared for a moment at
the network of fine silver threads underlying the
flesh, and, with three careful twists of the scalpel's
edge, altered the thermostatic control in his body.

He shivered a moment as his metabolism rolled
with the adjustment; then, gradually, he began to feel
warm. Closing the wound, he applied nuplast; moments later, it had healed. He dressed again.

He surveyed his room. Twenty feet square, with a
bed, a desk, a closet, a dresser. There was a small
air conditioning grid mounted in the ceiling. The usual
plates provided a steady greenish electroluminescent
glow. There was an oval window, beneath which was
a set of polarizing controls. There was a molecular
bath and washstand. It was neither the shabbiest nor
the most elegant room he had ever stayed in. It
wasn't bad for twenty units a week, he told himself,
trying to think the way an Earthman might.

The room-calendar told him it was half past three
in the afternoon, 22 May 2562. He was not supposed
to make contact with Central for ten days or more.
Closing his eyes, he pictured the Terran calendar and
computed that that would mean the first week of
June. Until then he was simply acting the part of a
Terran on vacation.

The surgeon had made certain minor alterations in his metabolism to give him a taste for Terran food and drink and to make it possible for him to digest the carbohydrates which the Terrans were so damnedly fond of consuming. They had prepared him well for playing the part of Major Abner Harris. And he had been equipped with fifty thousand units of Terran money, which was enough to last him quite a while.

Carefully he adjusted the device on the door to keep intruders out while he was gone. Anyone entering the room surreptitiously now would get a nasty jolt of energy, not enough to kill but enough to annoy. Harris checked his wallet, made sure he had his money with him, and pushed the door-opener.

It slid back and he stepped through, into the hallway. At that moment someone walking rapidly down the hall collided with him, spinning him around. He felt a soft body pressed against his.

A woman!

The immediate reaction that boiled up in him was one of anger, but he blocked the impulse to strike her before it rose. On Darruu, a woman who dared to jostle a Servant of the Spirit could expect a sound whipping.

But this was not Darruu.

And he remembered a phrase from his indoctrination: *it will help to create a sexual relationship for yourself on Earth, by way of camouflage.*

The surgeons had changed his metabolism in that respect, too, making him capable of feeling sexual desires for Terran females. The camouflage theory held that no one would expect a disguised alien being to engage in romantic affairs with Terrans; it would serve as an effective bit of sidetracking.

"Excuse me!" said Harris and the female Terran in the same instant.

His training reminded him that simultaneous outbursts by two people were cause for laughter on Earth. He laughed. So did she.

Then she said, "I guess I just didn't see you. I was hurrying along the corridor and I wasn't looking."

"The fault was all mine," Harris insisted. *Terran males are obstinately chivalrous*, he had been instructed. "I opened my eyes and just charged out blind. I'm awfully sorry."

He looked at her. She was tall, nearly his height, with soft, lustrous yellow hair and clear pink skin. She wore a black body-tight sheath that left her shoulders and the upper hemispheres of the breasts uncovered. Harris found her attractive.

Wonderingly he thought, *Now I really know the surgeons have changed me. She has hair on her scalp, and enormous bulging breasts, and yet I can feel desire for such a creature!*

She said, "It's my fault and it's your fault both. That's the way most collisions are caused. Let's not argue about it." She threw him a dazzling smile. "My name is Beth Baldwin."

"Major Abner Harris."

"Major?"

"Interstellar Development Corps."

"Oh," she said. "Just arrived on Earth?"

He nodded. "I'm here on vacation. My last stint was Alpheratz IV." He grinned and said, "You know, it's silly to stand out here in the hall discussing things. I was on my way down below to get something to eat. How about joining me?"

She looked doubtful for a moment, but only for a moment. Then she brightened.

"I'm game," she said.

They took the gravshaft down and ate in the hotel's third-level restaurant, which was an automated affair with individual conveyor-belts bringing food to each table. Part of his hypnotic training had been intended to see him safely through social situations such as this, and so he ordered a dinner for two, complete with wine, without a hitch.

She did not seem shy. She told him that she was employed on Rigel XII, and had come to Earth on a business trip. She had arrived only the day before. She was twenty-nine, she said, unmarried, a native-born Earther like himself. She had been living in the Rigel system for the past four years, she finished.

"And now tell me about you," she said, reaching for the wine decanter.

Harris shrugged diffidently. "There isn't very much to tell, I'm afraid. I'm a fairly stodgy career man in the IDC, age forty-two, and this is the first day I've spent on Earth in ten years."

"It must feel strange."

"It does."

"How much vacation do you have?"

He tapped his fingertips together. "Six to eight months. I can have more if I really want it. When do you go back to Rigel?"

She smiled strangely at him. "I may not go back at all. Depends on whether I can find what I'm looking for on Earth."

"And what, pray tell, are you looking for?"

She chuckled lightly. "That's my business," she said with finality.

"Sorry."

"Never mind the apologies. Let's have some more wine."

After Harris had settled up the not inconsiderable matter of the bill, they left the hotel and went outside to stroll a while. The streets were crowded; a clock atop a distant building told Harris that the time was shortly after seven in the evening.

He felt warm, now that he had adjusted his temperature controls. The unfamiliar foods and wines in his stomach gave him an oddly queasy feeling, though he had enjoyed the meal.

The girl slipped her hand through his looped arm and squeezed the inside of his elbow in an affectionate way. Harris smiled at her.

He said, "I was afraid it was going to be a terribly lonely vacation."

"Me too. You can be tremendously alone on a planet that has nine billion people living on it."

"Especially if you're a stranger on your own world," he said glibly. "Having been away for ten years."

They walked on. In the middle of the street a troupe of acrobats was performing, using nullgrav devices to add to their abilities. Harris chuckled and tossed them a coin, and a bronzed girl saluted to him from the top of a human pyramid.

Night was falling. Harris considered the incongruity of walking arm-in-arm with an Earthgirl, with his belly full of Earth foods, and enjoying it.

Darruu seemed impossibly distant now. It lay eleven hundred light-years from Earth; its star was visible from here only as part of a mass of blurred dots of light, without individuality.

But yet he knew that it was there. And he missed it.

"You're worrying about something," the girl at his side said.

"It's an old failing of mine."

He was thinking: *I was born a Servant of the Spirit, and so I was chosen to go to Earth. I may never return to Darruu again.*

As the sky darkened they strolled on, over a delicate golden bridge airly spanning a river whose dark depths twinkled with myriad points of light. Together they stared down at the water, and at the stars reflected in it. She moved closer to him, and her warmth against his body was strangely pleasing to him.

Eleven hundred light-years from home.

Why am I here?

He knew the answer, of course. Titanic conflict was shaping in the universe. The Predictors held that the cataclysm was no more than two hundred years away. Darruu would stand against its ancient adversary Medlin, and all the worlds of the universe would be ranged on one side or on the other.

He was here as an ambassador. Earth was a mighty force in the galaxy—so mighty that it would resent the role it was scheduled to play, that of pawn between Darruu and Medlin. Darruu wanted, needed Terran support in the conflict to come. Obtaining it would be a delicate problem in the art of engineering consent.

A cadre of disguised Darruui, planted on Earth, gradually manipulating public opinion toward the Darruu camp and away from Medlin—that was the plan, and Major Abner Harris, born Aar Kiilom, was one of its agents.

They walked through the city until the hour had grown very late, and then turned back toward the hotel. Harris was thoroughly confident now that he had established the sort of relationship with the girl that was likely to shield him from all suspicion of his true origin.

He said, "What do we do now?"

"Suppose we buy a bottle of something and have a party in your room?" she suggested readily.

"My room's a frightful mess," Harris said, thinking of the many things in there that he would not want her to see. "How about yours?"

"It's all right. It doesn't matter."

They stopped at an autobar and he fed demi-unit pieces into a gleaming machine until the chime sounded and a fully wrapped bottle slid out of the receiving tray. Harris tucked it under his arm, made a mock-courteous bow to the girl, and they continued on their way to the hotel.

The signal came just as they entered the lobby.

It reached Harris in the form of a sudden twinge in the abdomen; that was where the amplifier had been embedded. He felt it as three quick impulses, *rasp, rasp, rasp,* followed after a brief pause by a repeat.

The signal had only one meaning: *There is an emergency. Get in touch with your contact-man at once. Emergency!*

Her hand tightened on his arm. "Are you all right? You look so pale!"

In a tense voice he said, "Maybe we'd better postpone our little party a few minutes, Beth. I'm— not quite well."

"Oh! Is there any way I can help?"

He shook his head. "It's something I picked up on Alpheratz," he said huskily. Turning, he handed her the packaged liquor bottle and said, "It'll just take me a few minutes to get myself settled down. Suppose you go to your room and wait for me there."

"But if you're sick I ought to . . ."

"No. Beth, I have to take care of this myself, without anyone else watching. Is that okay with you?"

"Okay," she said doubtfully.

"Thanks. Be with you just as soon as I can."

They rode the gravshaft together to the 58th floor of the hotel and went their separate ways, she to her room, he to his. The signal in his abdomen was repeating itself steadily now with quiet urgency; *rasp rasp rasp. Rasp rasp rasp. Rasp rasp rasp.*

He neutralized the force-field on the door with a quick energy impulse and opened the door. Stepping inside quickly, he activated the spybeam jammer again. Beads of cold sweat were starting to form on his skin.

Rasp rasp rasp. Rasp rasp´rasp.

He opened the closet, took out the tiny narrow-beam amplifier that he had hidden there, and tuned it to the frequency of the emergency signal. Immediately the rasping within him ceased as the narrow-beam amplifier covered the wavelength.

Long moments passed. The amplifier picked up a voice speaking in the code devised for use among Darruui agents alone.

"Identify yourself."

Harris identified himself according to the regular procedure. He went on to say, "I arrived on Earth today. My instructions were not to report to you for about two weeks."

"I know all that," was the impatient reply. "There's an emergency situation."

"What's the trouble?"

"We've discovered there are Medlin agents on Earth. Normal procedures will have to be altered. I want you to meet me at once."

He gave an address. Harris memorized it and repeated it. The contact was broken.

Meet me at once. The orders had to be interpreted literally. *At once* meant right now, not tomorrow afternoon at Harris' convenience. His tryst with the yellow-haired Earthgirl would just have to wait.

He picked up the housephone and asked for her room. A moment later he heard her voice.

"Hello?"

"Beth, this is Abner Harris."

"Are you all right? Is everything under control? I'm waiting for you."

Hesitantly he said, "I'm fine now. But . . . Beth, I don't know how to say this—will you believe me when I tell you that a friend of mine just phoned, and wants me to meet him right away, downtown?"

"Now? But it's after eleven!"

"I know. He's a strange sort. Keeps odd hours. I've got to go."

"I thought you didn't have any friends on Earth, Major Harris. You said you were lonely." Her voice was sharp with the edgy sarcasm of disappointment.

"He's not really a *friend*," Harris said uncomfortably. "He's a business associate. From IDC."

"Well, I'm not accustomed to having men stand me up. But I guess I don't have any choice, do I?"

"Good girl. Make it a date for breakfast in the morning instead?"

"It's a lousy substitute, but it'll have to do. What time?"

"Oh, nine."

"All right," she said. "See you at nine, Major Harris."

Three

He stopped in the hotel lobby and poked his nose into the concierge's booth. The concierge, a bony-faced, hawk-nosed man whose veiled eyes glittered with the knowledge accumulated in a hundred years of hotel-iering, smiled subserviently at him.

"Yes?"

"I'd like to know how to get to 11543 Narvon Boulevard, the quickest way."

A grin creased the leathery face. "The Major is interested in the night-life, is he? Have you made a reservation? The Narvon Boulevard clubs usually have few empty seats."

"I'm meeting a friend there," Harris said. "I assume he's taken care of the arrangements. Is it possible to walk there?"

"To walk? Oh, no, no, not advisable at all. It is a very long walk. And not at all safe. I will get a helitaxi for you. It is a very quick trip by helitaxi."

Harris nodded and slipped a bill into the cubicle. The concierge picked up a phone and spoke briefly into it. "The helitaxi will be here in a moment, Major. If you will be so kind as to wait by the north entrance of the hotel . . ."

Harris stepped outside. Another uniformed flunkey pointed to the helitaxi ramp curving upward at the right. Harris mounted it, and moments later a gleaming helitaxi settled down, its generators purring, and a door irised open in its flank.

Harris got in.

"Narvon Boulevard, Major?" the cabbie said.

"That's right."

Harris leaned back against the plush upholstery. The sound of sinuous music filtered down from the small speaker in the cab's roof. There was the sudden throb of powerful rotors, and then they were aloft, rising vertically to the thousand-foot level.

The ride was a short one, eastward out of the heart of the city. They passed from the region of bright lights to one of dimness, and then to another area of brightness, this time gaudy and flamboyant rather than merely warm and brilliant.

The helitaxi spiralled downward onto a public landing ramp.

"Three units fifty," the cabbie said.

Harris peeled off four units and got out. The cab whirred off into the mild night, leaving him alone.

The other operative had named a specific streetcorner as their rendezvous point. Harris walked up to the corner, where a coolfire streetsign glowed a lambent green against the side of a building, and discovered that he was on the 105 block of Narvon Boulevard. He had to go to the 115 block. Somebody had given the cabbie the wrong instructions, he thought in annoyance. Walking ten blocks in the dark didn't overly much appeal to him.

He started to walk. It was a nightclub district, all bright lights and brassy music. From time to time he spied stealthy figures moving off down dark alleyways between the clubs, but he kept moving, secure in the knowledge that he was armed and could handle himself in all but the most unexpected of attacks.

The blocks peeled away. 106 block, 109, 113. Each was like its predecessor—an unending strip of amusement palaces and honky-tonks. Judging from the radiant signs outside, each had its own specialty— nude dancing girls in one, gambling in the next, exotic liqueurs in the next, darker things perhaps in some.

He reached the 115 block.

A figure leaned casually against the lamppost on the southeast corner of the street. Quickly Harris crossed to him. In the brightness of the streetlamp he was able to make out the other's face: lean, lantern-jawed, solemn, with a grave dignity to it.

Harris walked up. The other man regarded him with blank lack of interest.

Harris said softly, "Pardon me, friend. Do you

know where I might be able to purchase a mask for the carnival, by any chance?''

It was the agreed-upon recognition-query. The other answered, in a deep, harsh voice, ''Masks are expensive. You would be wiser to stay home.''

He thrust out his hand.

Harris took it, gripping the wrist in the Darruui manner, and rejoicing in the contact, in the firm grasp of the other man. Eleven hundred light-years from home and he beheld a fellow Servant of the Spirit! His depressing load of lonely homesickness dropped away.

''I'm Major Abner Harris,'' he said.

The other nodded. ''Good to meet you. I'm John Carver. There's a table waiting for us inside.''

''Inside'' turned out to be a place that called itself the Nine Planets Club, across the street. The atmosphere inside was steamy and smoke-clouded; bubbles of coolfire drifted round the ceiling, half a dozen colors of it that gave a rainbow effect to the greasy clouds of smoke. A row of long-limbed nudes pranced gaily to the accompaniment of the raucously discordant noise that passed for music on Terra. The surgeons, Harris thought, had never managed to instill a liking for Terran music in him, whatever other wonders they had succeeded in performing.

A bar-girl came over. She was a Rigelian megamastid, exceptionally well endowed, practically exploding out of her scanty yellow tunic. She flashed a synthetically voluptuous smile whose cynicism turned

Harris' stomach and said, "What'll it be to drink, boys?"

Carver answered, "A Nine Planets Sling."

"And you?"

Harris hesitated. "Make it the same," he replied after a moment.

The girl stalked away, her bosoms swaying. Harris said, "What have I just ordered?"

"It's all the rage this year. You'll see."

The Nine Planets Sling turned out to be something cloudy and cool in a tall glass brimming with ice. Harris tasted it, and found it musky but not unpleasant. It seemed to be a mixture of half a dozen different liquors and some sort of fruit juice. He sipped it slowly.

Carver said in a low voice, "Have you had any trouble since you arrived?"

"No. Should I have been expecting any?"

The lean man shrugged inconclusively. "Trouble is brewing. It may come any day."

"What sort of trouble?"

"There are one hundred Medlin agents on Earth right now," Carver said. "Yesterday we stumbled onto an important cache of secret Medlin documents. Now we have the names of the hundred and their photographs. We also know that they plan to wipe us out in the very near future."

Harris bit into a lump of ice and chewed it reflectively. "How many Darruui are on Earth right now?" he asked.

"You are the tenth to arrive."

Harris' eyes widened. He hadn't thought the situation was as bad as all that. One hundred Medlins here already, against only ten Darruui!

"Stiff odds," he said.

Carver nodded. "Agreed. But we know their identities, while they are ignorant of ours. We can strike first. We *must* strike first. Unless we eliminate them, we will not be able to proceed with our work here."

The music reached an ear-splitting crescendo. Moodily, Harris stared at the nude chorus-line as it gyrated. Strangely, he felt some glandular disturbance at the sight of the girls, and frowned. Was his Earthman's outward form betraying him? There was no reason for him to be aroused by those cavorting girls. By any Darruui standards, the girls were obscenely ugly.

But this was not Darruu.

He tightened his grip on his nearly empty glass and said, "How do we go about eliminating these hundred Medlins?"

"You have weapons. I'll supply you with the necessary information. You know the odds. If you can manage to get ten of them before they get you—and if each of the rest of us can do the same—we'll be all right." Carver drew a billfold forth from his tunic and extracted a snapshot from it with lean, edgily nervous fingers. "Here's your first one, now. Kill her and report back to me. The job should be easy because she's staying at the Spaceways Hotel, the same as you."

Harris felt a jolt. "A Medlin at my hotel?"

"Why not? They're everywhere. Here. Take a look at the picture."

Harris accepted the photo from the other Darruui and scanned it. It was a glossy tridim in natural color. It showed a blonde girl wearing a low-cut black sheath. The shot seemed to have been taken by a hidden camera at some sort of party. The girl was laughing and waving a cocktail glass in the air, and other figures could be seen behind her in the picture.

Controlling his voice, Harris said, "This girl's much too pretty to be a Medlin agent."

"That's why she's so deadly," Carver said. "Kill her first. She goes under the name of Beth Baldwin."

Harris stared at the photo a long while. A pulse pounded in his forehead, and a strange swirl of emotions rushed through his brain. This girl? A spy? He thought back over the day, the pleasant time he had had with her, the feeling of warmth, of friendship. *Kill her first*, Carver had said.

"Something the matter, Major?"

"No. Not at all."

"You look very . . . preoccupied."

"It's just a reaction from my travelling," Harris said. He handed the incriminating photo back to Carver and nodded his head. "Okay. The assignment has been received. I'll get in touch with you again when the job's done."

"Good. Another drink?"

Harris was uncertain. The first one had left him a bit giddy, and vaguely ill at ease in the pit of his stomach. His Darruui metabolism was not really comfortable handling these alien hydrocarbons.

But he nodded abruptly. "Yes. Yes, I think I'll have another."

It was nearly two in the morning when Harris returned to his hotel. He had spent something over an hour with the man who called himself John Carver. Harris felt tired, confused, wan. He found himself faced with decisions that frightened him, here at the very outset of his tour of duty on Earth.

Beth Baldwin a Medlin spy?

How improbable that seemed! But yet Carver had had her photo. Could there have been some mistake? No. Carver would not make a mistake on a matter like that. Beth had been definitely identified as a spy, or else Carver would not have given the assassination order.

And it was Harris' job to kill her, now—a task he had no option of refusing. He was a Servant of the Spirit. He could not betray his trust.

But before he committed himself to any irrevocable course of action, he told himself, he would do a little checking in advance. Carver might not be infallible. He did not want the blood of an innocent to live as a blemish on his soul.

He took the gavshaft to the 58th floor, but instead of going to his own room, he turned left and headed down the corridor toward the room whose number Beth Baldwin had given him—5820.

He paused a moment outside her door, then nudged the door-signal.

There was no immediate response. He frowned and nudged it again. This time he heard the sound of a door-scanner humming just above him, telling him that she was awake and just within the door.

He said, "It's me. Abner. I have to see you, Beth."

"It's late. It's the middle of the night."

"I'm sorry if I woke you. It's important that I talk to you."

"Hold on," came the sleepy reply from inside. "Let me get something on, Abner."

He waited. A moment passed, and then the door slid silently open. Beth smiled at him warmly. She had "put something on," all right, but the "something" had not been very much. She had donned a flimsy gown that concealed her body as if she were wearing so much gauze.

But Harris was not interested in the contours of her body now, attractive though that body happened to be. He was staring at the tiny glittering weapon that she held firmly in her hand, trained on his skull.

Harris recognized the weapon.

It was the Medlin version of the disruptor-pistol.

He had the confirmation he had come to get. But he had not expected to gain it this way.

"Come on in, Abner," she said in a coolly calm voice, gesturing with the disruptor.

Numbly he stepped forward, too stunned to speak.

The door shut behind him. Beth pointed toward a chair with the disruptor's snout.

"Sit down over there."

He ran his tongue over dry lips. "How come the gun, Beth?"

"You know that answer without my having to tell it to you," she said. "Will you sit down?"

He sat.

She nodded. "Now that you've been to see Carver, you know exactly who I am."

"He said you were a Medlin agent. I was skeptical, but . . ." He glanced at the gun.

It was hard to believe, but the proof was staring menacingly at him. He looked at the lovely girl who stood only ten feet away from him, holding a disruptor trained at his brain. Judging from her appearance, the Medlin surgeons were as skillful as those of Darruu, it seemed, perhaps even more skilled, for the wiry pebble-skinned Medlins were even less humanoid than the Darruu—and yet he would have taken an oath on his birth-tree that those breasts, those flaring hips, those long well-formed legs, were genuine and not the product of the surgeon's arts. Certainly they looked as genuine as was conceivable.

Disconcertingly genuine.

The Medlin who called herself Beth Baldwin said, "We had complete information on you from the moment you entered the orbit of Earth, Abner—or should I rather say, Aar Khiilom?"

He started in surprise. The jolt of hearing his own

name spoken on Earth was like getting a bucket of icewater in the face.

"How did you know that name?" he demanded.

She laughed lightly. "I knew it the same way I knew you were from Darruu, the same way I knew the exact moment you were going to come out of your room before, when we collided."

"So that was arranged?"

"Of course."

"And you also knew in advance that I was coming here to kill you just now?"

She nodded.

Harris frowned and considered the situation. "Medlins aren't telepathic," he said doggedly. "There isn't a single telepathic race in the galaxy."

"None that *you* know about, anyway," she said, a mocking light dancing in her eyes.

He tensed. "What do you mean by that?"

"Nothing. Let it pass."

He shrugged the idea away. Apparently the Medlin spy system was formidably well organized, perhaps utilizing a traitor or two on Darruu itself. All this nonsense about telepathy was a false lure she was setting up merely to cloud the trail. But the one fact about which there was no doubt whatever was . . .

"I came here to kill you," Harris said. "I bungled it. You trapped me. I guess you're going to kill me now, eh, Beth?"

"Wrong. I just want to talk," she said.

He eyed her thoughtfully, and began to relax just a little. He said in a flat voice, angry with her now for this cat-and-mouse treatment, "If you want to talk, have the good grace to put some clothing on, will you? Having you standing around wearing next to nothing disturbs my powers of conversation."

"Oh?" she said, laughing in a silvery, brittle way. "You mean this artificial body of mine stirs some response in that artificial body of yours? How quaint! How very interesting!" Without turning her back on him or lowering the disruptor, she drew a robe from the closet and slipped it on over the filmy gown. "There," she purred. "Is that easier on your glandular balance?"

"Somewhat."

"I wouldn't want you to be in any discomfort on my account," she said.

The Darruui began to fidget. She was toying with him, making a mockery of him. The more he recalled of their earlier conversation, of his mawkish, almost maudlin talk of loneliness and homesickness, the more he detested her for having fooled him this way—though he had to admit his motives had not been of the purest either.

He was deeply troubled, now. There was no way he could possibly activate his emergency signal without moving his hands, and any sudden handmotion was likely to be fatal so long as Beth kept that disruptor angled down on him. He sat reluctantly motionless while rivers of sweat streamed down the skin they had grafted to his own.

"So you have me," he said. "What do you want with me? Why don't you kill me and get it over with?"

"You must think I'm terribly cruel."

"You're a Medlin."

"I admit that much. Are the words 'Medlin' and 'cruel' synonymous in your vocabulary, Abner?"

"Our worlds have been enemies for centuries. Am I supposed to admire the nobility of the Medlins? Their lofty intelligence? Their physical beauty? Your world is a world of jackals and murderers!" he spat out.

"How kind of you, Abner."

"Pull the trigger and get it over with!" he raged. "I won't be taunted this way."

She shrugged. "I still prefer to talk."

"Talk, then," he muttered.

Beth said, "Very well. I'll tell you what I know about you. You're one of ten Darruui on Earth. Other agents are on their way from Darruu now, but at the moment there are only ten of you here. Correct me if I'm wrong."

"Why should I?" Harris said tightly.

She nodded. "A good point. You're under no obligation to betray your people. But I assure you that we have all the information about you that we need, so you needn't try to make up tales for the sake of patriotism. Don't strain your imagination. To continue: you and your outfit are here on Earth for the purpose of subverting Terran allegiance and winning Earth over to the side of Darruu."

"I won't deny that," Harris said. "But you Medlins are here for much the same kind of reason—to get control of Earth."

"That's where you're wrong," the girl said sharply. "We're here to help the Terrans, not to dominate them."

"Oh, of course."

"You can't understand motives like that, can you?" she asked, a cutting edge of scorn in her voice.

"I can *understand* altruistic motives well enough," he said easily. "I just have trouble believing in altruism when it's preached by a Medlin."

She scowled. "I suppose you'll think it's more propaganda when I tell you that we Medlins don't believe in violence if peaceful means will accomplish our goals."

"Those are very nice words," Harris said. "They'd look good inscribed on a monument of galactic harmony. But how can you help the Terrans?"

"It's a matter of genetics."

"I don't understand."

"I didn't expect you to. But this isn't the time or the place to explain in detail."

He let that point pass. In a bitter voice he said, "So you deliberately threw yourself in contact with me earlier, let me take you out to dinner, walked around arm-in-arm, and all this time you knew I was actually a Darruui in disguise?"

"Of course I knew."

"Wasn't it cynical of you to talk and act the way you did?"

"And what about you?" she shot back at him. "Taking advantage of an innocent Earthgirl? Feeding her a lot of lies about yourself?"

"It's different," he said lamely.

"Is it?" She laughed. "I also knew that when you were pretending to get sick earlier this evening, it was really because you had to contact your chief operative. And I knew that when you told me you were going to visit a friend, you were actually attending an emergency rendezvous. I also knew what your friend Carver was going to tell you to do—which is why I had my gun ready when you came ringing at my door."

He stared at her. "Suppose I *hadn't* gotten that emergency message, though. Suppose I had no idea of what you really were. We were going to come here to your room and drink and probably make love. Would you . . . would you have gone to bed with me, even knowing what you knew?"

She was silent a moment.

Then she said, without emotion, "Most likely. It would have been most interesting to see what sort of biological reactions the Darruui surgeons are capable of building."

A flash of savage, blind hatred rippled through Harris-Khiilom. *The bitch!* he thought. He had been raised to hate Medlins anyway; they were the ancient ancestral enemies of his people, galactic rivals of the Darruui for four thousand years, perhaps more. The mere sight of a Medlin was enough to stir rage in a Darruui. Only the fact that this one was clad in the flesh of a handsome Earthgirl had kept Harris from feeling his normal revulsion for all things Medlin.

But now it surged forth at this revelation of her

calm and callous biological "curiosity." It was almost blasphemous for someone so lovely to speak so
hideously.

He wondered how far her callousness extended. If
he made a move, would she gun him down?

And how good was her aim?

Probably too good, especially at point-blank range.
He mastered his anger and said, "That's a pretty
cold-blooded way of thinking, Beth."

"Maybe. I'm sorry if my frankness offends you."

"I'll bet you are."

She smiled at him and said in a gentler voice,
"Let's forget about that, shall we? There are a few
things I want to tell you."

"Such as?"

"For one: did you know that you're fundamentally
disloyal to the Darruui cause?"

Harris laughed harshly, thinking with fierce nostalgia of his homeland.

"You're crazy!"

"Afraid not. Listen to me, Abner, and see if I'm
not telling the truth. You're desperately homesick for
Darruu, aren't you?"

"Admitted."

"You never wanted to come here in the first place,
but the assignment was given to you, and you took it.
You happened to have been born into a caste that has
certain obligations of public service imposed on it,
and you're fulfilling those obligations. But you don't
really know very much about what it is you're doing
here on Earth, and for half a plugged unit you'd give

the whole thing up and go back to Darruu on the next ship out.''

''Very clever,'' he said stonily, inwardly realizing the truth of her words, though refusing to let her see that. ''Now give me my horoscope for the next six months,'' he said in a tone of heavy sarcasm.

''That's easy enough. First, you'll come to our headquarters and learn what my people hope to accomplish on Earth . . .''

''I know that one already.''

''You *think* you do,'' she said smoothly. ''But all you really know is what your own propaganda ministers have told you. Don't interrupt. You'll learn the real reason why we're on Earth. Once you've come to see what that is, you'll join us and help to protect Earth against the menace represented by Darruu.''

He laughed. ''I'll turn against my own world?''

''You will.''

''And why, precisely, are you so sure that I'll do all these incredible things?''

''Because it's in your personality makeup to do them,'' she said. ''You can't help doing them, once the right motivation is supplied. Besides, you're falling in love.''

''With you?'' Harris snapped. ''Don't flatter yourself, girl.''

''I'm speaking objectively. I know your own mind better than you do.''

''And you can stand there and tell me that I'm falling in love with a lot of fake female flesh plastered over a scrawny and repulsive Medlin body? Hah!''

She remained calm, still wearing that serene smile, and not replying.

Harris measured the distance between them, wondering whether she would use the weapon after all if he jumped at her. A disruptor broiled the neural tissue; if she got him in the brain or in any key part of the body, death would be instantaneous and fairly ghastly. Even a swiping shot across a limb would leave him crippled.

He decided to risk it.

He was a Servant of the Spirit, he reminded himself. He was here under certain obligations, as even the Medlin wench seemed to know. His assignment was to kill Medlins, not to let himself be killed by them. He had nothing to lose by making the attempt— and nothing but a scar on his soul to gain if he let her frighten him with that shiny little disruptor.

In a soft voice he said, "You didn't answer me, Beth—or whatever your name really is. Do you actually think I'd fall in love with something like *you*?"

"Why not?"

"Do Darruui and Medlins ever feel anything but hate for one another? Medlins are physically disgusting to all Darruui. You know that."

"Biologically we're Earthers now, not Medlins or Darruui. It's possible that there could be an attraction between us."

"Maybe you're right," he admitted. "After all, I *did* ask you to cover your body so it wouldn't distract me. And I reacted the same way to dancing girls in the night club with Carver." He smiled and said,

"I'm all confused. I need some time to think things over."

"Of course. You . . ."

He sprang from the chair and covered the ten feet that separated them in two big bounds, expecting at any moment to feel the searing blast of the disruptor frying his nervous system. He stretched out one hand desperately to grab the wrist of the arm that held the disruptor.

He succeeded in deflecting the weapon toward the ceiling. She did not even attempt to fire. He closed on her wrist, tightening until he could feel the delicate bones grinding against one another.

"Drop it!" he grated.

The tiny pistol dropped to the tiled floor. With a deft flick of his toe, Harris kicked the disruptor out of sight under the bed. Pressed against her, he stared into eyes blazing with anger.

The anger melted suddenly into passion as their bodies pressed tight. Automatically he tensed as he saw the warm, beckoning look in her eyes. Then a surge of cautious fear went through him.

She's trying to trap me with her body, he thought. *Taking advantage of these damned confused Earther sexdrives they built into me.*

He stepped back, not willing to have such close contact with her, afraid to let himself be lured.

He reached for his own gun. She was too dangerous to be allowed to live, he thought. Beautiful as she was, it was safer, wiser, to kill her right now, while he had the chance to do it. She's just a Medlin, he argued. A deadly one.

He started to draw the weapon from his tunic. Suddenly she lifted her hand, moved it in a quick arc upward. There was the twinkling of something bright glittering between her fingers.

She laughed.

Then Harris recoiled, helpless, as the bolt of a stunner struck him in the face like a club against the back of his skull. She had moved fast, much too fast for him. He had hardly even seen the motion as she pulled the concealed weapon from its hiding place.

She fired again.

He struggled to get his gun out, but his muscles would not obey.

He toppled forward, paralyzed.

Four

Harris felt a teeth-chattering chill sweep through him
as he began to come awake. There was a hammering
back of his eyeballs, and a sick hollowness in his
stomach. The stunner-bolt had temporarily overloaded
his motor neurons, and the body's escape from the
frustration of paralysis was unconsciousness.

Now he was waking, and the strength was ebbing
slowly and painfully back into his muscles. His entire
body felt drained, depleted.

The light of morning streamed palely in through
a depolarized window on the left wall of the unfamiliar room in which he found himself. He was
not bound in any way. He felt stiff and sore all
over, every muscle cramped and congested. He
wondered where he had spent the night. Not in any

bed, certainly. Probably right here on the cold floor of this room.

He put his hands to his forehead and pressed hard. The throbbing seemed to stop, but the relief was only momentary. It was no joke to be a stunnergun victim. He had been stunned only once before in his life, and that had been a glancing, accidental swipe during a training session. This had been a full-on charge, two shots. The stunner was considered a mild weapon, but the medicos claimed that the body couldn't stand more than two or three stunnings in any one year. An overdose of stunnings and the nerves just gave up entirely, the muscles stopped working in despair—including the muscle of the heart, and the muscles that work the lungs.

Harris got unsteadily to his feet and surveyed the room. The cell, rather. The window was high on the wall, beyond his reach, and covered over with a welded grid just to make escape even less possible. There was no sign of a door anywhere. Obviously some section of the wall folded away to admit people to the room—they hadn't jammed him in through that tiny window—but the door and door-jamb, wherever they might be, must have been machined as smoothly as a couple of jo-blocks, because there was absolutely no sign of a break in the wall.

He was trapped.

A fine fix for a Servant of the Spirit, he told himself bitterly. To be outmaneuvered by a girl—a Medlin girl at that—to get into a hopeless muddle of emotions; to be jumped and outdrawn; to let himself get stunned and captured; it was hardly a record to be proud of, he thought. His mission on Earth had certainly not gotten off to an auspicious start, though it might very well be coming to an unexpectedly rapid conclusion.

He looked up. There was a grid in the ceiling, circular, six or seven inches in diameter. The air-conditioning vent, no doubt—and probably it housed some spy-mechanism also, through which they could watch him and communicate with him.

He stared at the grid and said in a sour voice, "Okay, whoever you are. I'm awake now. You can come in and work me over."

There was no immediate response, other than a faint hum that told of an electronic ear within the grid. Surreptitiously, Harris slipped a hand inside his waistband and pinched up a fold of flesh between his thumb and index finger, squeezing it gently. The action set in operation a minute amplifier that was embedded there. A distress signal, directionally modulated, was sent out to any Darruui agents who might be within a thousand-mile radius. He completed the gesture by lazily scratching his chest, stretching, yawning.

He waited.

An endless two or three minutes ticked by. Then his attention was caught by a chittering sound in the wall, and an instant later a segment of the wall flipped upward out of sight in some clever way that he could not detect.

Three figures entered the cell.

Harris recognized one of the three: Beth. She had changed into a fresh, simple tunic, and she was smiling at him with genuine warmth, apparently untroubled by his attempt to murder her the night before.

"Good morning, Major," she said sweetly.

Harris glared bleakly at her, then looked at the other two who stood behind her.

One was an ordinary looking sort of Earther, an even-featured, forgettable kind of man just under middle height. The other was rather special, Harris saw. He stood about six feet eight or even taller, well-proportioned for his height, with a regularity of feature that seemed startlingly beautiful even to Harris' Darruu-oriented viewpoint.

Beth said, "Major Abner Harris, formerly Aar Khiilom of Darruu, this is Paul Coburn of Medlin Intelligence." She indicated the Earther of undistinguished appearance.

"How do you do?" the Medlin who called himself Paul Coburn said blandly, putting out his hand.

Harris studied the hand disdainfully without taking it. He knew the meaning of a handshake on Earth, and he was damned if he'd shake hands with any Medlin intelligence operators.

Beth seemed unbothered by Harris' lack of civility. She indicated the giant and said, "And this is David Wrynn, of Earth."

"A real home-grown-native-born Earthman?" Harris asked sardonically. "Not just a laboratory-made phony like the rest of us?"

Wrynn smiled pleasantly and said, "I assure you that I'm a completely domestic product, Major Harris." His voice was like the mellow boom of a well-tuned cello, and his smile was so piercingly friendly that it made Harris uncomfortable.

The Darruui folded his arms and glared. "Well. How nice of you to introduce us all. Now what? A game of cards? Chess? Tea?"

"Still belligerent," he heard Beth murmur to the other Medlin, Coburn. Coburn nodded and whispered something in return that Harris could not catch. The giant Earthman merely looked unhappy in a serenely unruffled way.

Harris eyed them all coldly and snapped, "Well, if you're going to torture me, why not get started with it and not waste so much time?"

"Who said anything about torture?" Beth asked.

"Why else would you bring me here? Obviously you want to wring information from me. Well, go ahead," Harris said. "Do your worst. I'm ready for you."

Coburn chuckled and fingered the soft rolls of flesh under his chin. "Don't you think that we're well aware how useless it would be to torture you?" he asked mildly. "That if we tried any kind of neural entry to your mind, your memory-chambers would automatically short-circuit out?"

Harris' jaw dropped in shock. "How did you ever find out . . ."

He stopped. The Medlins evidently had a fantastically efficient spy service, he thought shakenly. The filter-circuit in his brain was a highly secret development, known only to Darruui surgeons and agents.

Beth said, "Relax and listen to us, will you? We aren't out to torture you. I mean that seriously. We already know all you can tell us."

"Doubtful. But go ahead and talk."

"We know how many Darruui are on Earth, and we know approximately where they are."

"Really, now?"

"There are ten of you, aren't there?"

He kept his face expressionless. Were they bluffing him to test their own guesses, or did they really know? He shrugged and said, "Maybe there are ten and maybe there are ten thousand."

"There are ten," Beth said. "Ten and no more. It happens to be the truth. Only ten."

"Perhaps."

"One of the ten is right here—you. A second one is also in this city—Carver. The other eight are scattered. We have a particular job in mind for you, Major. We'd like you to seek out your nine comrades, to be a contact man for us."

"To what end?"

"To the end of killing the other nine Darruui on Earth," Beth said simply.

Harris smiled. It was laughable that they could ask him so earnestly to commit high treason, as though they thought that by simple rational persuasion they could get him to change sides. Were they just fools, or were they playing some devilishly subtle game with him?

"Is there any special reason," he asked slowly, "why I should seek out my friends and comrades and murder them for you?"

"For the good of the universe."

He laughed derisively. "An abstraction is the last refuge of an idiot. For the good of the universe? You think that has any meaning? You want me to do it for the good of Medlin, you mean. It'll be easier if I kill them than if you do—you won't have it on your pretty consciences and so you're asking me to . . ."

"No," Beth said. "Will you listen to me and let me explain?"

"I'm waiting. It had better be a damned good explanation."

She ran her tongue lightly over her lips. Much as he despised her, Harris thought, he was still painfully affected by her physical beauty. Her synthetic beauty, he told himself—but the argument had no effect.

Beth said, "When we arrived on Earth—it was a good many years ago, by the way—we explored the situation and made a surprising discovery. We found out that a new race was evolving here, a new type of Earthman. A super-race, you might say. A breed of Earthmen with abnormal physical and mental powers.

"But in most cases children of this new race were killed or mentally stunted before they reached maturity. They were out of tune with the species around them, and their very apartness caused trouble for them. Often they felt the need to prove themselves in some way—and swam ten miles out to sea and couldn't get back. Or they pushed their extraordinary reflexes too far even for them—raced automobiles dangerously, climbed murderous mountains, and so on. Some of them committed suicide out of sheer loneliness. Some were murdered by the normals, murdered outright, or crippled emotionally by parents who were jealous of the child they had brought into the world. People tend to resent being made obsolete—and even a super-child is unable to defend himself until he's learned how. By then it's usually too late.''

It was a nice fairy-tale, Harris thought idly. He made no comment, but listened with apparent interest.

Beth went on, ''Despite all the handicaps, these mutants continued to crop up. It was a persistent genetic constellation, but we realized that unless enough members of the new species could be allowed to live to maturity, to meet others and marry, the mutation would wither and drop back into the pool of genes that didn't make it.

''We discovered isolated members of this new race here and there on Earth, scattered in every continent. We decided to *help* them—knowing they would help us, some day in the future, when we would need them to stand by us. So we sought them out. We found the super-children, and we protected them. It had to be done subtly, because we ourselves were interlopers on Earth and couldn't bear the risk of exposure. But it worked. We got the children away from their parents, we brought them together, we raised them in safety."

Beth pointed at the giant. "David Wrynn here is one of our first discoveries."

Harris glanced at the big Earthman. "So you're a superman?" he asked bluntly.

Wrynn smiled. With a diffident shrug he said, "I'm somewhat better equipped for life than most other Earthmen, let's say. I can't fly by flapping my arms, I can't hold my breath for two hours under water, but I'm an improvement in the breed all the same. My children will be as far beyond me as I am beyond my parents."

Beth said earnestly, passionately, "Do you see, Harris? Can you get the Darruui blinkers off your eyes and understand? Our purpose here on Earth is to aid this evolving race until it's capable of taking care of itself—which won't be too long, now. The species is reaching the self-generating stage. There are more than a hundred of them, of which thirty are adults. But now, in the middle of our work, Darruui agents have started to arrive on Earth. They've carried the long rivalry between our worlds to this planet, which doesn't want any part of our struggle. And the Darruui purpose is to obstruct us, to interfere with our actions, and to win Earth over to what they think is their 'cause.' They aren't smart enough to understand that they're backing a dead horse."

Harris stared at her levelly, wondering how much of a fool she really thought he was. Finally he said, "Tell me something honestly."

"Everything I've said has been honest. What do you want to know?"

"What's your motive in bringing this super-race into being?"

Beth shook her head. "Motive?" she said. "You Darruui always think in terms of motives, don't you? Profit and reward, *quid pro quo*. Major, can you understand what I'm talking about when I tell you that there's nothing in this for us at all?"

"Nothing?"

"Nothing but the satisfaction of knowing we're helping to bring something wonderful into being in the universe, something that wouldn't exist without our help and encouragement."

Harris swallowed that with a goodly ration of salt. The concept of pure altruism was not unknown on Darruu, certainly, but altruism had its limits. It seemed highly improbable that a planet would go to all the trouble and expense of sending emissaries across space for the sole purpose of serving as midwives to an emerging race of Terran super beings.

No, he thought.

It didn't hold up to close scrutiny.

This whole fantastic story of hers was simply part of an elaborately conceived propaganda maneuver whose motives did not lie close to the surface.

There were no supermen, Harris thought. Wrynn was tall and handsome, but there was nothing about him that could not be accounted for in the normal distribution curve of Terran physiques. For that matter, he might not be an Earthman at all, Harris reflected—in all probability Wrynn was a Medlin himself, on whom the surgeons had done an especially good job.

Harris could not fathom the scheme's depths. But whatever the Medlins' motives, he made up his mind to play along with them and go where it led him. By this time, Carver had almost certainly picked up his distress signal and most likely had calculated the location of the place where he was being held.

Harris said cautiously, "All right. So you're busily raising a breed of super-Earthmen, and you want me to help."

"Yes."

"How?"

"We told you," Beth said. "By disposing of your nine Darruui comrades. Getting them out of the way before they make things more complicated for us than they already have become."

Harris said levelly, "You're asking me with straight faces to commit high treason against my people, in other words."

"We know what sort of a man you are," Beth said. "We have—techniques. We know you, Aar Khiilom. We know that you aren't in sympathy with the imperialistic ideals of the Darruui ruling council. You may *think* you are, you may have brainwashed yourself into thinking so, for your own safety on Darruu, but you really aren't. You've got the stuff of a traitor in you. And I don't mean that as an insult. I mean it as the highest compliment I know how to give a member of your race."

I'll play along, Harris thought.

He said, "You know, you people are so perceptive it frightens me."

"How so?"

"You see with clear eyes. I don't even understand my own motivations, but you do. When they sent me here I was unsure of what I was doing. I didn't know what advantage it was to Darruu to gain Earth's sympathies. All I knew was I had to block the Medlin thrust. A blind, negative reason for journeying here. And now—now I'm not so sure about the values I've put so much blind faith in . . ."

"Will you join us?" Beth asked.

Harris paused. "I might as well admit it. You're right. I didn't want to take the Earth assignment in the first place, but I had no choice. I begin to see that I'm on the wrong side. What can I do to help?"

Coburn and Beth exchanged glances. The "Earthman" Wrynn merely smiled.

Have I overplayed my hand? he wondered. *Did it seem too obvious, too plainly phony? Maybe I should have held out a while longer before seeming to jump sides.*

But Beth said, "I knew you'd co-operate, Major."

"What's my first assignment?"

"Target number one is the man who calls himself John Carver. Once you get rid of him, the other Darruui agents are without a nerve-center. After him, the other eight will be easy to nip."

"How do you know I won't trick you once you've released me?" Harris asked.

Coburn said, "We have ways of keeping watch over you, Major."

He didn't elaborate. Harris simply nodded and said, "All right. I'll go after Carver first. I'll get in touch with you as soon as he's out of the way."

Five

They marched him out of the room and led him into a gravshaft that rose, rather than fell. Up, up, out of who knew what subterranean depths under the city. He pondered the "sunlight" he had thought he saw coming through the barred window, and realized that he had deceived himself. The gravshaft shot upward endlessly, until he came to a halt with an abrupt jiggle and slid open to discharge him onto the main level of an enormous office building.

He stood for a moment in the crowded lobby. Earthers and aliens of all descriptions were busily going through the grand concourse. Slowly, Harris walked toward the nearest exit, and out into the noisy, bustling street. It was still fairly early in the morning, and the day was mild and sunny.

There was a streetguide mounted against a wall half a block from where he had emerged. He walked to it and peered at the crosshatched lines of the city map. At first he had difficulty getting his bearings. A red circle marked his present location, but none of the streets rang in his memory. Only when he glanced completely across the map did he discover the section of the city where his hotel was located.

They had taken him miles from the hotel, then. He fed a small coin into the slot and punched out coordinates as the sign instructed, and a glowing light illuminated the path from his present site to the hotel. It was, he guessed, at least an hour's journey by helitaxi from here.

He walked on. The spirals of a public helitaxi ramp gleamed yellow in the early sunlight not far ahead. He passed an open-air cafe, and the smell of newly baked bread and fresh coffee clawed at his stomach. But, hungry as he was, he knew he had no time to bother about breakfast until he had gotten in touch with the Darruui chief agent and passed the story along. A waiter came out and smiled at him hopefully, pointing to a vacant curbside table, but Harris shook his head and moved on.

He thought about Beth Baldwin and her words.

It seemed too transparent, too much of a strain on his credulity. All this talk of supermen and altruism, of fledgling mutant races that had to be coddled along and protected from the jealous furies of their obsolescent ancestors!

It made no real sense, Harris thought. Nothing that

he knew of Medlin psychology led him to believe they would make themselves parties to any such absurd project. If anything, he reasoned, the Medlins would take quick steps to throttle any upsurge of new and potentially dangerous abilities among the Terrans. As would the Darruui, had they been the ones to discover the alleged mutants.

It was only a simple matter of self-preservation, after all. Supermen represent super-dangers. The universe was a precarious enough place as it was, without standing by complacently while new races came into being. Those that existed now were well enough balanced, strength for strength, in an uneasy but oddly comforting stalemate. Only madmen would allow an X factor to enter the situation—and only very deranged madmen indeed would actually help bring the X factor about.

No, he thought, there were no supermen. The idea made no sense at all—Medlin propaganda was devious stuff, and he had good reason to mistrust it.

Were they as simple as all that, though, to release him merely on his promise of good faith? After all, they knew his murderous intentions. Only some sort of sleight-of-hand on Beth's part had saved her from death last night. And yet they had released him on his bland say-so of co-operation, after he had snapped and snarled at them for half an hour in scorn. If they were truly altruistic, it made sense, since in his lexicon pure altruists and pure fools were synonymous. But he knew the Medlins too well to swallow the idea that they could be as simple-minded as all that.

Darkly he thought that they were using him as part of some larger Medlin plan.

Well, let Carver worry about it, he thought. It was his responsibility to form strategy and to meet Medlin challenges.

Harris reached the helitaxi ramp. A taxi was ready for takeoff, but a plump, pink-faced citizen of obvious self-importance scuttled past the Darruui, his green cape fluttering pompously behind him, and pressed his bulk into the car. Shrugging, Harris signalled for another. It whirred up the ramp and the door opened.

"Where to, Colonel?"

"Spaceways Hotel. And I'm only a Major," he said, slipping back into character. "Thanks for the promotion, though."

"Any time, Major."

Powerful generators thrummed. The taxi lifted off and sought its level, under instructions from the master computer somewhere far beneath the city. Harris closed his eyes and settled back against the faintly acid-smelling cushion. The taxi was old, well worn. He listened to the droning of the computer voice.

He had never dreamed a city could be so huge. On Darruu, the size of cities was limited by an age-old statute to three million persons, and no city exceeded that. Of course, since all the planned urban formations had been developed for millennia, it meant that population was fairly stabilized. No new cities had been founded on Darruu for fifteen hundred years. All of the present cities had their maximum population quota. If you wanted to move to another city, you had to get a permit. That wasn't so difficult, since there were always enough people moving back and forth to cancel out and keep each city at the statutory limit of three million.

But if you wanted to have a child—ah, that was something different. That had to be balanced against the death rolls, and death did not come early on Darruu. There were couples who had waited out their entire fertility span in fruitlessness without getting a permit, because of an uptick in longevity.

That did not concern Aar Khiilom. As a Servant of the Spirit he did not have the right to reproduce himself. It was a sacrifice he freely made.

He did not question the system. It was a good one, he thought. It kept the planet stable, it encouraged emigration to the colony worlds, and it avoided helter-skelter urban scrambles of the kind he was experiencing now. He felt a sense of revulsion as he peered from the helitaxi ports at the city below, the endless city, the city of twenty or thirty or perhaps even fifty million humans, the city that stretched in gray rows to the horizon.

It was inconceivable to him that a city should have such distances that one could travel for fifty minutes by helitaxi within it. And he had not even gone from border to border. No, he had simply journeyed from a point near the southeast limb of the city to one near the heart of the city—and it had been nearly an hour's trip, which meant a distance of hundreds of miles.

They were coming down, now.

The taxi swung in narrowing circles onto the landing ramp of the Spaceways Hotel. Harris paid the driver and headed straight into the hotel, and up to his room.

He activated the narrow-beam communicator, and waited until the metallic voice from the speaker said in code, "Carver here."

"Harris speaking."

"You've escaped?"

"Not exactly. They set me free of their own accord."

"How'd you work that?"

"It's a long story," Harris said. "Did you get a directional fix on the building where they were holding me?"

"Yes. Why did they let you go?" Carver persisted.

Harris chuckled. "At their urging, I promised to become a Medlin secret agent. My first assignment," he said pleasantly, "is to assassinate you."

The answering chuckle that came from the speaker grid held little mirth. Carver said, "Is this some kind of joke?"

"The gospel."

"You agreed to assassinate me?"

"First you, then the others."

Carver paused. "All right, Harris. Fill me in on everything that's happened to you since I saw you at the club last night."

"I went back to the hotel," Harris said. "I went to the Baldwin girl's room, intending to remove her.

But she was ready for me, ready and waiting. When she answered the door she had a disruptor in her hand.''

"*What?*"

"The Medlins know everything, Carver. But *everything*. They're one step ahead of us all the way. I got the gun away from the girl, but she had a stunner on her and she let me have it. She said she'd been keeping tabs on me from the start, that she knew why I was here, that she knew about every phase of the Darruui mission here. Carver, there's been a leak."

"Impossible."

"Is it? Listen, they know how many of us there are. She told me to my face that there are ten Darruui agents on Earth."

"A lucky guess," Carver scoffed.

"Maybe. But she knew my name. *She knew my name, Carver!* She called me Aar Khiilom! Was that a guess too?"

There was an instant of silence at the other end.

"Carver? I don't hear you."

"There's no way she could have known that," Carver said puzzledly. "No documents she could have captured anywhere that would give that away."

"I tell you, they know everything. They know about the cut-off memory circuit too."

"Impossible. Flatly impossible that they should know a thing like that."

Harris began to feel impatient with his superior. Restraining his temper, he said as evenly as he could, "Do you choose not to believe me?"

"I believe you. But I don't understand."

"You think I do?"

"Very well. What else happened to you last night?"

"After she stunned me, she carted me off to the Medlin headquarters. It's a sub-surface building far on the other side of town. When I woke up she introduced me to two staff members. A disguised Medlin named Paul Coburn and an oversized Earther who calls himself David Wrynn."

"Coburn is on our list," Carver said. "He's Medlin Intelligence. I don't know anything about this Wrynn. He is probably an Earthman as he says."

Harris said, "The girl started giving me some weird line about raising a breed of super-Earthmen." Quickly he repeated the story Beth had told about the supposed species of mutants. "They asked me if I would help them in this noble cause."

"You agreed?"

"Of course I agreed," Harris said. "They let me go and sent me out to handle my first assignment for them."

"Which is?"

"I'm supposed to eradicate all the Darruui on Earth, beginning with you."

"The others are well scattered," Carver said.

"The Medlins seem to know where they are. The Medlins seem to know every phase of our operation from top to bottom. You'd better start hunting for that security leak, Carver. One of your men's been selling us out."

Carver was silent for a moment. Then he said,

"There's only one thing we can do now. We'll have to accelerate the program and strike at once. Surprise may overcome the disadvantages we're under. We'll attack the Medlin headquarters and kill as many of them as we can. Do you really think they trust you?"

"It's hard to tell. I'm inclined to think that they don't trust me at all, that they're using me as bait for an elaborate trap," Harris said.

"That's more likely. Well, we'll take their bait. Only they won't be able to handle us once they've caught hold of us."

"Don't underestimate them, Carver."

"I'm not. But don't underestimate our strength either. Don't underestimate yourself, Harris. Remember that we're Servants of the Spirit. Doesn't that count for something? What are a hundred Medlins against us, after all?"

Harris closed his eyes. His body throbbed with hunger, and at the moment, having had some demonstration at close range of Medlin abilities, he was not so buoyantly imbued with religious faith as was Carver.

He said noncommittally, "Yes. Yes, we must keep that in mind."

Carver broke contact. Carefully Harris packed the equipment away again, watching it slither into the tesseract and vanish.

A prolonged session under the molecular showerbath was the next item on the agenda. The soothing abrasion of the dancing molecular particles not only ground away the grime of his night's imprisonment, but rid his body of the poisons of fatigue, leaving him better able to face up to the new challenges the Medlins posed.

Breakfast came next. Dressing in a crisply laundered fresh uniform, he rode downstairs to the hotel restaurant and had a terran-style breakfast of fruit juice, hot rolls, bacon, coffee. For all his hunger, the meal was close to tasteless to him. The harsh acids of fear rolled in his digestive tract.

Returning to his room, he locked himself in, and threw himself wearily on the bed. He was a tired man, and a deeply troubled one.

Supermen, he thought.

He rolled the argument around in his mind for the hundredth time in the last two hours.

Did it make sense for the Medlins to rear and nurture a possible galactic conqueror?

No, no, an infinity of times, no!

Earthmen were dangerous enough as it was, without laboring long and mightily to enhance their powers. Though the spheres of galactic influence still were divided as of old between Darruu and Medlin, the two-edged blade that had sundered the universe for millennia, the Earthmen in their bare three hundred years of galactic contact with the older races had taken giant strides toward holding a major place in the affairs of the universe.

Three hundred years was only a moment in galactic history. It had taken ten times that long for Darruu to reach outward and plant colonies. The active phase of the Darruu-Medlin conflict had gone on for nearly as long as the entire dominant culture-group of Earth had been in cohesive existence. The present, or inactive phase of the conflict, had begun when Earthers were still using animal-drawn vehicles for transportation.

Yet a slim three centuries had gone by since the first Earther ship broke the barrier of light, and in the time since then they had planted colonies halfway across the galaxy, stretching on to the dim reaches of the star cluster. The Interstellar Development Corps, of which he in the guise of Abner Harris claimed to be a member, had planted colonies of Earthmen indiscriminately on any uninhabited and habitable world of the galaxy that was not claimed by Darruu or Medlin—including some that both the older races had written off as uninhabitable by oxygen-breathing species.

And the Medlins, the ancient enemies of his people, the race that he had been taught all his life to regard as the embodiment of evil—these Medlins were aiding Earthmen to progress to a plane of development far beyond anything either Darruu or Medlin had attained?

Ridiculous, he thought.

No race knowingly and enthusiastically breeds its own destruction, not even a race of fools. And the Medlins were anything but fools.

Certainly not fools enough to let me get out of their hands on nothing but a mere promise that I'll turn traitor and help them, he thought.

He shook his head in bewilderment.

After a while he rose, got his precious flask of

Darruui wine, uncorked it, poured a small quantity out into a glass. He held the glass in the palm of his hand a long moment without drinking it, warming the wine so that he could inhale the bouquet.

Finally he lifted the wine to his lips and allowed himself a grudging sip. It was almost unbearable to taste the velvet-textured dark wine of his homeworld again. It soothed him a little, but the ultimate result was simply to increase beyond toleration his already painful longing for home.

He closed his eyes and pictured the vineyards of Moruum Tiira, ripening slowly in the crimson mists of summer. He had been born in the wine country. He remembered the cellars of his grandfather's house, with the casks of wine a century old and more, ranged in dusty rows. Only on special occasions were those casks disturbed. On the day of his coming of age, they had let him sip wine that was young when the Earthers were still planetbound. On the day of the trimming of his birth-tree, his grandfather let him taste the tongue-searing pure brandy he distilled.

On the day of his adoption into the ranks of the Servants of the Spirit, the wine had flowed freely too. Old wine, new wine. A joyous night, that one had been, a night never to forget.

Now, on Darruu, the grapes hung heavy on the vines, swelling with sugar, ripening, almost ready to ferment. Soon it would be harvest-time, and then weeks afterward the first bottles of new wine would reach the shops, and in Moruum Tiira there would be the days of thanksgiving, when wine flowed like water in praise of the Spirit that had granted the summer's blessings, and women gave themselves to all without stint, and happiness reigned.

This would be the first year, he realized, that he had not tasted the new vintage while it still held the bouquet of youth. On Darruu they would be gathering to pronounce the verdict on this year's vintage. But they would do it without him. He would not share that time of happiness this year, and perhaps never again would he know the joys of vintage time. Others back home would have the delights.

While I find myself on a strange planet, wearing a strange skin, and caught up in the toils of the devil Medlins, he thought.

He scowled darkly, and took another sip of wine to ease the ache his heart felt.

Six

A day of nerve-twisting inactivity passed, moment by endless moment.

Harris did not hear from Carver, though he waited all morning for a message. Nor did any of the Medlins contact him. Toward midday, Harris went down the hall to Beth Baldwin's room, but when he signalled no one answered the door.

In the lobby, he checked at the desk. "I'd like to leave a message for Miss Baldwin," he said.

"What room is that, sir?"

"5820."

The clerk checked the board. "I'm sorry, sir. That room was vacated earlier this day."

Harris drummed on the desktops with his finger-tips, and noted in grim amusement that he was even acquiring the Terran gestures of irritation and impatience. "Did she leave a forwarding address?"

Another check of the board.

"No, sir, I'm sorry but she didn't."

Harris sighed. "All right. Thanks anyway, I guess."

He walked away. It figured, he thought, that she would have severed all links this way. She had established quarters in the hotel only long enough to come into contact with him. Her mission accomplished, she had left without leaving a trace.

Regretfully, Harris wished he had had a chance to try that biological experiment with her, after all. The thought struck him as faintly perverse, since she was a Medlin under the curving flesh. But, Medlin though she might be, his body was now Terran-oriented, his entire glandular system rearranged and modified, and it might have been an interesting experience.

Well, there was no chance for that now. And just as well, he decided. Consorting with the enemy was a crime and a sin against the Spirit no matter what sort of bodies were being worn by whom.

Wearily, he left the hotel, feeling the need for some fresh air and exercise. On Darruu it had been his custom to swim eight lengths every morning, winter or summer, redmist or pinkmist. Here, in this concrete monster of a city, there was no chance for that, and his atrophying muscles ached from neglect.

He walked instead.

He walked down narrow streets two thousand years old, through winding alleyways that led down to the river, stinking and polluted, that wound through the core of the giant city. He stood at the river's edge, on the paved embankment, looking out at the sluggishly flowing water rolling toward the sea. The sky was thick with helitaxis, not with seabirds. The bustle of commerce was everywhere.

This Earth was a rich world, he thought. A world of shopkeepers, of merchants, of financiers and thieves. There were no spiritual values here, not even a decent sense of military discipline. Earth was a curious mixture of the ruthless and the spineless, and Harris was at a loss to understand the culture.

The river's stink oppressed him. He turned away, gagging, and made his way back into the interior. Jostling robocarts thrummed by him on all sides. He was troubled by the swarming omnipresence of people, busy people. Nine billion people on a single world, and a small world at that—it was a numbing thought. And yet, he understood that there were still vast tracts of Earth where no one lived at all—open wastelands and jungle lands that still had not been developed, though settlements were beginning to nibble at their edges.

The Earthers preferred to lump themselves together in huge cities, and to let the outlands rot. Why? Why these mind-blasting conurbations?

Were they afraid to be alone?

Harris shrugged. This world gave him a choking feeling. He would be well glad to be rid of it, to be back on Darruu again, to see an open field and to smell clean air, to revel in the tang of cold water against his naked skin in the hours after dawn.

He passed a building so sleek its sides were mirrors of stone. His face, hardly distorted, peered back at him. Not his face, not Aar Khiilom's face, but Abner Harris'. He was starting to forget what he had looked like. Aar Khiilom of the city of Helasz was a stranger to him now. He closed his eyes for a moment, saw his old face, red-eyed, golden-hued, hairless, with angular cheekbones jutting up harshly to cast his eyes into shadow.

Someday he would have that face back, he told himself hopefully. They would strip away the pink overlay, remove the obscene mat of bestial hair that sprouted on it, rip out the cheek-padding that hid the knifelike blades of his cheekbones. The surgeons would restore his tendrils. They would no longer be functional ones, no longer would give him advance warning of changes in barometric pressure, but that had been a small enough sacrifice. A Servant of the Spirit must be prepared to yield up not merely his tendrils but his eyes, his heart, his life, even, if Darruu requests it of him. With the privileges of nobility come the obligations as well, and he had never questioned that.

But he longed for Darruu.

He longed for his own face.

Carver is right, he thought. *We must strike fast, wipe out the scheming Medlins. And then home! Home to Darruu!*

As the afternoon shadows began to gather, Harris returned to the hotel, and ate alone in the hotel restaurant. He found he had little appetite, and he ate simply, avoiding the more exotic aspects of the hotel's menu. As a place that catered to a largely interstellar clientele, they featured delicacies from all corners of the universe—at least, all corners of the universe where Terran tradesmen were active. There was nothing Darruui on the menu, nothing even from a planet near Darruu, and Harris had no taste at the moment for dishes of other alien worlds.

After eating, he returned to the room and lay down on his bed. Automatically, he assumed a Darruui position of comfort—on his back, legs in the air, knees flexed—but realizing that he might be under a spybeam, he caught himself and stretched out into a conventional Terran repose-position. He tried to relax.

Toward evening, his signal-amplifier buzzed. Reaching across, he activated the communicator.

"Harris here."

"Carver. Rendezvous time in one hour."

"Where?"

"8963 Aragon Boulevard," Carver said. "We meet on the eighth floor."

Harris repeated the address. Carver signalled off. Feeling a rising sense of excitement now that the long day of boredom had ended, Harris rose, dressed, armed himself, and went out.

He hired a helitaxi, gave the driver the address. The driver squirmed around in his seat and said, "What's that address again?"

"Aragon Boulevard. 8963."

"Damned if I know where *that* is. Hold on and let me get computer direction."

Harris waited. It was an impossible city, he thought angrily. Imagine cab drivers unable to find their way around! The city was too big, of course, but that had nothing to do with the immediate problem. Why couldn't they have a systematic arrangement of the streets? Hadn't they heard of city planning on Earth? Didn't they know what a street grid was? Why did they have to name their streets, instead of numbering them?

An absurd planet, he thought.

But, he realized, with all their inefficiencies and irrationalities, these Earthers had managed to forge outward into the galaxy at a faster pace than any other species in the history of sentience. That was a chilling thought. What, he wondered, would these people be capable of if they were actually functioning at full efficiency?

What would they be like when the new super-Earthmen evolved into domination?

He began to shiver apprehensively. He cursed the Medlins anew. Had they no sense? Couldn't they see what a menace they were spawning?

The helitaxi lifted. Harris settled back, tried to calm himself. The situation was coming under control. In short order the Medlins would be eliminated, and then there would be nothing to fear from Earth and its new race.

Aragon Boulevard, for all its grand-sounding name, turned out to be a crooked, dusty excuse for a street far to the east, at the edge of the river. There was not even a helitaxi ramp in sight, and the cabbie had to let him off in the middle of a plaza some blocks away.

Harris trudged through gathering darkness toward the 8900 block, and found the building, shabby and old-fashioned, weatherbeaten and worn. There was no one on duty in the lobby. He simply walked in and made his way toward the gravshaft.

He rode up eight stories in a creaking antique of a gravshaft that vibrated so badly he expected to be hurled back down at any moment, and made his way down a dusty, poorly-lit corridor to a peeling, frayed door that gave off the faint hiss and yellow glow that indicated the presence of a protection-field.

Harris felt the gentle tingling in his stomach that told him he was getting a radionic scanning. He waited patiently.

Finally the door opened.

"Come in," Carver said.

Harris stepped inside. There were four others in the room, besides himself and the Darruui leader. Carver said, speaking carefully in Terran as though determined not to make use of his Darruui background in any way, "This is Major Abner Harris, gentlemen."

The other four introduced themselves in turn—a pudgy, balding man named Reynolds; a youthful, smiling one who called himself Tompkins; a short, cold-eyed man who gave his name as McDermott; and a lanky, lean fellow who introduced himself drawlingly as Patterson. As each of them in turn gave his name, he made the Darruui recognition signal, and Harris acknowledged it.

"The other four of us are elsewhere in the eastern hemisphere of Earth," Carver said. "But six should be enough to handle the situation."

Harris glanced at his five Darruui comrades. They looked run-of-the-mill, ordinary. Of the group, only he, with his crisp uniform and stiff military bearing, would seem capable to an outsider of being able to handle any kind of situation.

But he knew that that was a superficial way of assessing their strength. These five had been *designed* to look unobtrusive and unheroic. Beneath their Terran exteriors, all five were Servants of the Spirit, and so reliable to the utmost in any crisis.

"What are your plans?" Harris asked Carver.

"As discussed yesterday. We're going to attack the Medlins, of course. We'll have to wipe them out at once, down to the last of them."

Harris nodded. But to his own surprise he felt troubled and dismayed. The image of Beth Baldwin, dead by his hand, crossed his mind. Frowning, he tried to clear his brain of such treacherous thoughts. But despite his earlier conviction of the need to destroy the Medlins, it seemed to him now that they had been strangely sincere in releasing him.

He knew that that was preposterous. He dismissed the idea from his mind.

"How will we wipe them out?" he asked.

"They trust you," Carver said. "You're one of their agents now, as far as they know."

"Right."

"You'll return to them and tell them you've disposed of me, as instructed, and are reporting for your next assignment. Only you'll be bearing a subsonic on your body. We'll implant it now. Once you're inside the headquarters, you activate the subsonic and knock them out."

"And knock myself out as well?"

"No," Carver said. "You'll be fully shielded."

"I see," Harris said. "Then I'm supposed to . . . kill them when they're unconscious?"

"Exactly," Carver said.

The fat man, Reynolds, said slowly, "It would seem to me that there is a trace of reluctance on the Major's face, yes?"

Harris fought to get his rebellious features to wear a properly patriotic, dutiful expression.

McDermott said, "Perhaps the Major has some lingering emotional feelings about one of the Medlins?"

Harris flashed a furious look at him. Was he that transparent, he wondered? Could they all fathom him so easily?

Carver said, "Is there anything troubling you, Major Harris?"

"No."

"You're completely willing to carry out the assignment?"

"I am a Servant of the Spirit," Harris said stiffly.

Carver nodded. "So you are. I should not have

questioned your motives even by implication." There seemed to be more than a trace of mockery about his tone, Harris thought. Carver went on, "You know, you can't be humane with Medlins, Harris. It's axiomatic, I'd say. It's like being humane with blood-sucking bats or with snakes."

Harris felt tremors running through his legs. Five pairs of Darruui eyes were fixed balefully on him.

What are they thinking? Do they suspect me of something? Maybe they think I really have sold out to the Medlins!

The Darruui called McDermott said, "We'll wait outside the Medlin headquarters until we get the signal from you telling us that you've done the job. If you need any help, just let us know."

"How does the plan strike you?" Carver asked.

Harris moistened his lips and tried to look soldierly. This sudden access of weakness troubled and bewildered him. He had never reacted this way before, even in much greater stress situations. "It sounds like it'll work," he said thinly. "It sounds all right."

"Very well," Carver said curtly. "I'm glad you approve. Reynolds, insert the subsonic."

Harris watched impassively as the bald man produced a small metal pellet no larger than a tiny bead, from which three tantalum filaments projected. With his body already a mass of surgically implanted devices, Harris was stoically ready for one more.

"Your trousers, Major . . ."

Harris dropped them. Reynolds drew a scalpel from

a case in his pocket, and, kneeling, lifted the flap of nerveless flesh on Harris' left thigh that served as trapdoor to the network of devices underneath.

Looking down curiously, Harris stared into the dark recesses of his own leg, eyeing the coiling hardware that lived there. Reynolds inserted two fingers and uncoiled a packet of wires.

Harris winced, holding himself rigidly in check as a searing wave of hellish pain rocked him.

"Sorry, Major," Reynolds said casually, untwisting the wires. "Hit the cortical centers that time, didn't I? Won't let it happen again."

Harris did not reply. The pain was receding slowly, leaving a residue of aches, but it was not his place to protest. He watched as with steady, unquivering fingers Reynolds affixed the bead to the minute wires already set into Harris' leg, and closed the wound with nuplast. Harris covered himself again. He felt only a faint itching where the fleshy trapdoor had been opened.

Carver said, "You activate it by pressing against the left-hip neural nexus. It's self-shielding for a distance of three feet around you, so make sure none of your victims are any closer than that. It won't work during an embrace, for instance."

Harris met the suggestion with a blank stare.

Reynolds said, "You'll find that it radiates a pretty potent subsonic. A guaranteed knockout for a radius of forty feet."

"Fatal?"

"Not to complex organisms. It'll kill anything less than a primate, though."

"And suppose the Medlins are shielded against subsonics?" Harris asked.

Carver chuckled confidently. "This is a variable-cycle transmitter, Major. If they've perfected anything that can shield against a random wave, we might as well give up right now."

"They've shown some other very surprising abilities," Harris pointed out.

"I'm inclined to think they'll be incapable of shielding against this," Reynolds said. "It would take technology of an overwhelmingly high order—an inconceivably high order—to work out any defense against a subsonic. The very simplicity of the device makes it impossible to counteract. Shall we test it?"

"We'd better," Carver said.

Reynolds gestured, and Tompkins and Patterson disappeared into one of the other rooms, returning with three cages containing some small Terran mammals. Harris did not recognize any of the species, but none looked to be of any high order of intelligence.

"We'll go down the hall," Carver said. "We'll signal you when we're out of range, and you see how your subsonic works."

Harris nodded tightly. The five Darruui left the room. Harris stared at the animals in the cages, and small beady eyes stared back at him, almost seeming to comprehend what he was about to do.

"All right!" Carver called from the distance.

Harris hesitated a moment. Then his hand slipped to his hip, and he pressed inward.

He felt nothing.

But the animals in the cage began to writhe and scream in sudden agony.

The smaller ones suffered least. For them, the pain ended quickly, and they slumped to the floor of their cages, tails twitching for a moment, small feet outstretching rigidly, claws grasping air for a moment and then going stiff.

The larger ones fought the subsonic more sturdily. Then they, too, succumbed, toppling with soft thuds, curling grotesquely into imitations of sleep.

Harris took his hand from his hip. He walked toward the cages, opened one, thrust his fingers in. He touched the small furry cadavers, felt only stiffness and death. Eyes that had been beady a moment before now looked unnaturally glossy as they peered unblinkingly out at him, accusingly.

"Well?" Carver yelled.

"It worked," he said. "You can come back in now! It's all over!"

The five Darruui filed back into the room. Reynolds took the animals from the cages and examined them.

"Dead," he said. "Every one."

"But it won't kill human beings?" Harris asked.

"It'll only stun them," Reynolds told him. "Even at close range. It's impossible to design a subsonic that can kill other human beings without killing its carrier in the bargain."

"And they can't shield against it?"

"No," Carver said. "The only way to defend against it is to key the shield to the random cycles, as your shield is keyed. But how can they do that? You can't fail, Harris. That's a guarantee."

Seven

One at a time, the six Darruui agents filed out into the streets and scattered. Harris had to walk almost a mile before he emerged from the bleak, deserted warehouse district and found an area civilized enough to have a helitaxi ramp. He reached his hotel shortly before midnight, and, ravenous, ordered a meal sent to his room.

As he undressed for bed, he studied his hip and thigh. There was no sign of anything unusual in either place, he saw. But yet he was equipped very efficiently to stun anyone who came within forty feet of him. If he had been so equipped the other night, Beth Baldwin would be dead by now, and none of this would have happened.

Just as well, he realized. It was only by being

captured that he had learned of the true extent of the Medlin operation on Earth. If he had simply killed Beth outright the first night, Darruu would have no hint of the real purpose of the Medlin agents.

He switched off the light.

He slept, but not well.

In the morning, he rode across town to the Medlin headquarters, far to the southeast. Everything was arranged well enough. The helitaxi let him off several blocks from the building, and, as he waited on the crowded corner, he watched the Darruui group assemble.

There was Carver, leaning against a lamppost and reading a newspaper.

Reynolds, gazing into the window of a wineshop diagonally across the street.

McDermott, pacing up and down before a bank and staring at his wristwatch every few minutes.

Patterson, browsing peacefully in a bookstall.

Tompkins, standing by the display of some open-air huckster trying to sell household appliances.

It was all innocent enough. The five of them were well spaced, far from one another. No one could possibly link them. No one could possibly guess that those five were alien creatures in Earther skin.

In turn, each glanced up, looked at him, nodded, then went back to what he was doing. Harris made the Darruui recognition-signal and moved along to carry out his deadly assignment.

It was all so very simple, he thought as he walked

up the block to the building that housed the Medlin headquarters. Simply walk in, smile politely, make a little harmless conversation with the Medlins.

Then stun them all with the subsonic, and boil their brains with your disruptor.

He reached the Medlin headquarters building and paused outside it, thinking.

Around him, Earthmen hurried to their jobs. He looked up. The sky was blindingly blue, flecked here and there with white fleece. But behind the peaceful blue of that sky lay the nightblack vault of space, and the burning orbs of the stars.

Many of those stars swore allegiance to Darruu. Others, to Medlin.

Which was right? Which wrong? Neither? Both?

A block away, five fellow Darruui lurked in seeming innocence, ready to come to his aid if he had any trouble in killing the Medlins. But he doubted that he would have trouble, if the subsonic was as effective and as foolproof as Carver seemed to think it would be. It had worked with chilling enough effectiveness on the test animals. But he had learned in the past few days not to underestimate the abilities of the Medlins.

For forty Darruui years, he had been trained to hate the Medlins, root and branch, man and child and babe in the womb. Now, in just a few more minutes, he would be doing what was considered the noblest act a Servant of the Spirit could possibly perform—ridding the universe of a pack of them.

Yet he felt no sense of anticipated glory. His deed

would be simply murder, nothing more glamorous than that. The murder of strangers in strange skins.

He entered the building.

He remembered this lobby all too well—the vast concourse, the arching ceiling high overhead, the crowd of Earthmen bustling past. He made his way to one of the Down gravshafts. The Earthers had run out of space in the upper reaches of their cities, having built a hundred and a hundred fifty stories high and daring to build no higher, and so they burrowed into the ground. This building rose ninety stories into the air, and dropped a hundred more into the sub-city bowels.

He rode down, down, down. The gravshaft's drop halted, finally. He got out, moved as in a dream down the by-now-familiar corridor toward the Medlin headquarters. It seemed to him that he could feel the pressure of the tiny subsonic generator in his thigh. He knew that it was only an illusion, a trick, but the presence of the metal bead irritated him all the same.

He stood for a moment in a scanner field in front of the Medlins' door. He expected to be questioned, but no questions came, and in a moment a door flicked back suddenly, out of sight, and a strange face peered at him—an Earthman face, on the surface of things, square-jawed and fleshy and deeply tanned.

The Earthman beckoned him in. Harris stepped through the door and felt it slice shut behind him.

"I'm Armin Moulton," the Earthman said in a deep voice. He did not put out his hand, nor did Harris offer his. "You're Major Harris?"

"That's right."

"We're glad you came. Beth is waiting to see you inside."

The last time he had been here, he had been too dazed, too numbed by the aftereffects of his stunning, to observe very much. Now he saw that the Medlin offices were capacious and extensive, with rooms going off in all directions. No doubt the cell in which they had kept him for the night was at the end of one of those corridors. The furnishings in the rooms were attractive and not inexpensive.

He followed Moulton inside.

He thought coldly, *The subsonic has a range of forty feet in any direction. It stuns but does not kill. No one should be closer to you than three feet. Your shielding protects you.*

He was shown into an inner room well furnished with colorful drapes and hangings. A warm light glowed from indirect sources.

Beth stood in the middle of the room, smiling at him. Today she wore thick, shapeless clothes, quite unlike the seductive garb she had had on when Harris first collided with her in that carefully prearranged and premeditated "accident" in the hotel corridor.

There were others in the room. Harris felt a coldness at the presence of so many of the enemy. He recognized the other Medlin, the plump pseudo-Earther Coburn, and the giant named Wrynn who claimed to be an Earthman of some new and superior species. There was another woman of Wrynn's size in the room, a great golden creature nearly a foot taller than

Harris, of breathtaking beauty and elegance. And there were two people of normal size who were probably Medlins in disguise.

"Well?" Beth asked.

In a tight voice Harris said, "He's dead. I've just come from there."

"How did you carry it out?" Beth asked.

"Disruptor," Harris said, keeping his voice in check. He saw several of the Medlins exchange glances. The two huge Earthers were regarding him with open, neutral expressions on their faces. Harris said, "It was . . . unpleasant. For me as well as for him."

"I imagine it would have been," Beth said.

He looked at her, wondering if he had succeeded in getting away with it. He was quivering with tension. He made no attempt to conceal it, since a man who had just killed his direct superior, and thus had committed high treason against his world, might be expected to show some signs of extreme tension.

"Eight Darruui to go," Coburn said, "And four are in another hemisphere."

"We know their location," Beth said. "We'll get them all in time. But first we'll concentrate on the others in this area. The ones who call themselves Tompkins, Patterson, McDermott, Reynolds."

Harris felt a chill. They knew every name! How did they know so much? Who was the traitor?

He looked around.

"Who are these people?" he asked, to break the tension. "You haven't told me their names."

Beth smiled apologetically. "I'm sorry. I was eager to find out how you had done." She pointed to the two normal-sized ones, and introduced them as disguised Medlin agents named Kranz and Marichal. The giant girl, Beth told him, was Wrynn's wife, a supergirl.

Harris frowned thoughtfully. There were a hundred Medlin agents on Earth, he knew. Four of them were right in this room, and it was reasonable to expect that two or three more might be at headquarters, within the forty-foot range of the concealed subsonic in his thigh. With luck, he might succeed in stunning and then killing as many as nine or ten of the Medlins on Earth.

Not a bad haul at all, he thought. Nearly ten percent of the whole Medlin complement in one swoop. And, two of these oversize Earthers. Reynolds and his scalpel would have to get to work on Wrynn and his wife once they were safely dead, Harris thought. Dissect them and see if Medlin gristle or Earther bone lay beneath their skins.

Suddenly Harris began to tremble.

Beth said, "I suppose you don't even know who and where the other Darruui are yourself, do you?"

"I've only been on Earth a couple of days, you know," Harris said, shaking his head. "There wasn't time to make contact with anyone but Carver. I don't even know the names of the other agents."

He stared levelly at her as he uttered the lie. The expression on her face was unreadable. It was impossible to tell whether she believed he had actually killed Carver, actually did not know the identities of his Darruui comrades on Earth.

"Things have happened fast to you, haven't they?" Beth said. She drew a tridim photo from a case and handed it to Harris. "This is your next victim," she said. "He goes under the name of Reynolds here. You'll find him right here in this city, I think. You should know how to make contact with him. He's the second-in-command in your group. First-in-command now, I suppose, since Carver's dead."

Harris studied the photo. The face of the fleshy, balding man who had inserted the subsonic beneath the skin of his thigh peered up at him. Reynolds, who was so close now.

Tension mounted in him.

He felt the faint *rasp rasp rasp* in his stomach. It was the agreed-upon code. Carver, waiting nearby, was buzzing to find out if he were having any trouble, needed any help.

Casually, Harris put his hand to his side, and kneaded the flesh with the heel of his palm, as though trying to ease the pain of an attack of indigestion. The signal he sent out told Carver that nothing had happened yet, that everything was all right. An acknowledging double buzz came from within.

Harris handed the photo back to Beth.

"Don't worry," he said. "I'll take care of him."

"You should be able to find him in a day or so," she said. "Make contact quickly and get him out of the way. There are still seven more after him, and we don't have much time to waste."

"I'll get him tomorrow," Harris vowed.

I press the neural nexus in the left hip and render them unconscious. Then I kill them all with the disruptor and leave.

Very simple.

In such easy ways do we win the Grace of the Spirit, he thought.

He looked at Beth, still radiantly lovely despite the deliberate glamorlessness of her clothing, and thought that in a few minutes she would lie here dead on the floor, as dead as those pitiful little glossy-eyed Terran animals in their cages. She would die, and Coburn, and the other two Medlins, and these giants who claimed to be Earthmen of some new super-species.

He tensed.

His hand stole toward his hip.

Then Beth broke the tension momentarily by saying, "Would you like to have a drink with us. Major? To celebrate your conversion to the forces of light?"

"No," he said. "I . . . I don't like liquor much . . ."

"Oh, really!" Beth laughed. "That isn't the impression I got the other night."

He frowned. Somehow it seemed even more blasphemous to take refreshment from these people and then to kill them. But they were putting him in an awkward position. Already, Coburn was producing a bottle and seven glasses. He began to pour a cloudy amber fluid. Gravely, he handed the glasses around until everyone in the room held one.

"What are we drinking?" Harris asked.

"Vriyl," Beth said. "It's a liqueur."

"An Earther liqueur?" he asked.

"No," she said with a pleasant smile. "A Medlin liqueur. We brought some with us."

Harris' hand shook so badly that he nearly spilled his drink. His stomach churned at the idea of drinking a Medlin beverage, of toasting with the enemy.

Beth saw the tremor and said, "It must have been a terrible nervous strain, killing him. You look extremely disturbed."

"You've overturned all the values of my life," Harris said glibly. "That can shake a man up."

Beth turned triumphantly to Coburn and said, "You didn't think I'd succeed!" To Harris she explained, "Coburn didn't think you could be trusted."

Coburn smiled uncomfortably. "Well, all that's past, now. Cheers, everyone."

Glasses went to lips. All but Harris'. He lifted his glass halfway, then gagged at the smell of the nauseous stuff and hurled liqueur and glass together to the floor. As the others looked at him in surprise, he said, "Coburn was right. I can't be trusted."

He activated the subsonic.

Eight

The first waves of inaudible below-the-threshold sound rippled out from the focus on his thigh, ignoring false flesh and striking through to the Medlin core beneath. Protected by the three-foot cone of his shield, Harris nevertheless felt sick to the stomach, rocked by the reverberating sound waves that poured from the pellet embedded in his thigh. Stabbing spasms of nausea shivered through him a dozen times a second.

But he was getting off lightly, compared with the others in the room.

Coburn, his face mottled by shock and anger, was reaching for his weapon, but he never got to it. Nerves refused to carry the messages of the angry brain. His arm drooped slackly. He slumped over, falling heavily to the floor.

Beth fell even more rapidly, dropping within an instant of the first waves.

The other two Medlins fell.

Still the subsonic waves poured forth, as Harris held his hand tightly to the nexus on his hip. To his surprise, Harris saw that the two giants were still remaining on their feet and were semi-conscious, if groggy. They were moving around in vague circles, shuffling and shambling, fighting the subsonic.

It must be because they're so big, he thought. *It takes longer for the subsonic to knock them out. I'll just have to keep juicing them for a while.*

Wrynn was sagging now, swaying from side to side like some wounded behemoth. His wife, reeling under the impact of the noiseless waves, slipped to the floor. A moment later her husband followed her, landing with an enormous booming thud as three hundred pounds of bone and muscle crashed to the floor.

The office was silent. Little puddles of darkness stained the carpet where the falling Medlins had spilled their drinks. Six unconscious forms lay sprawled awkwardly on the floor.

Harris pressed his side again, signalling the *all clear* to the five Darruui waiting in the street a block away.

He found the switch that opened the door and pulled it down. That uncanny mechanism whisked the door out of sight, and Harris peered outward into the hall. Three more Medlins lay outside, unconscious. A fourth was running toward them from the far end of the long hall. He was shouting, "What happened? What's going on? You people sick or something?"

Harris stared at him and pressed his hip a second time. The Medlin ran into the forty-foot zone and recoiled visibly, but without any awareness of what was happening to him. He staggered forward a few steps and fell, joining his comrades on the thick velvet carpet. Harris let the signal subside.

Ten of them, he thought.

Ten Medlins. Plus two more if the two giant Wrynns turned out not to be Earthers. A decent haul, he thought. A tenth of the Medlin task force blotted out in one simple operation.

He drew the disruptor.

It lay in his palm, small, deadly. The trigger was nothing more than a thin strand of metal. He needed only to flip off the guard, press the trigger back, aim casually in any direction, and watch the Medlins die of broiled brains and jellied synapses.

But his hand was shaking.

He did not fire.

He bit down hard on his lip and gritted his teeth and lifted the weapon, and tried to force himself to use it. But he could not. He raged at himself, scowled and harangued himself. This was no way for a Servant of the Spirit to behave! Those were Medlins down on the floor, beasts in human guise.

Kill them! Kill! *Kill!*

And he held the disruptor loosely, doing nothing. Sweating, he reached his left hand over, wrenched the guard off the disruptor. His finger curled into place over the trigger. He brought the gun up, pointed it at Beth, aimed it between her breasts. He closed his eyes and tried to strip away the deluding synthetic flesh, tried to carve the Medlin reality out of her, to reveal her as the hideous, pebble-skinned, bony monstrosity that he knew her to be beneath her Earther form. A muscle trembled in his cheek as he fought to pull the trigger and destroy her.

Then a silent voice within his skull whispered, *You could not be trusted after all, could you? You were a traitor through and through, a cheat and a liar. But we had to let the test go on at least to this point, for the sake of our consciences.*

"Who said that?" Harris gasped, looking wildly around in every corner of the room.

I did.

It felt like feathers brushing his brain. "Where are you?" he demanded, panicky. "I don't see you. Where are you hiding?"

I am in this room, came the calm reply, and Harris wanted to tear his skull apart to find the source of that quiet voice.

Put down the gun, Harris-Khiilom.

Harris hesitated. His hand moved an inch or two toward his bodily distress-signal. But even that gesture was intercepted, intercepted and understood.

No, don't try to signal your friends. Just let the gun fall.

As though it had been wrenched from his hand, the

gun dropped from his fingers. It bounced a few inches on the carpet and lay still.

Now shut off the subsonic, came the quiet command. *I find it unpleasant.*

Obediently, Harris deactivated the instrument. His mind was held in some strange stasis; he had no private volitional control whatever. His body throbbed with frustration. How were they doing this to him? They had made him a prisoner in his own mind.

His lips fumbled to shape words.

"Who are you? Tell me who you are!"

A member of that super-race whose existence you find it so difficult to accept.

Bewildered, Harris looked down at Wrynn and his wife. Both the fallen giants were unconscious, motionless, breathing slowly, regularly.

"Wrynn?" he asked hoarsely. "How can your mind function if you're unconscious?"

I am not Wrynn, came the reply.

"Not . . . Wrynn?"

No. Not Wrynn.

"Who are you, then? Where are you? Stop driving me crazy! I've got to know!"

I am not Wrynn, came the calm voice, *but Wrynn's unborn child.*

Gently Harris felt himself falling toward the floor. It was exactly as though an intangible, invisible hand had yanked his legs out from under him, then had caught him and eased his fall.

He lay quiescent, eyes open, neither moving nor wanting to move. He lacked even the power to sound his distress-signal. In some strange way the *desire* to call for help had been taken from him. Only in the depths of his mind did he boil with fear and frustration.

As the minutes passed, the victims of the subsonic slowly returned to consciousness.

Beth woke first. She sat up, stirred, put her hands to her eyes. She turned to the unconscious form of Wrynn's wife, and now Harris saw the gentle rounding of the giantess' belly.

Beth said to the unconscious giantess, "You went to quite an extreme to prove a point!"

You were in no danger, came the answer.

The others were awakening now, one by one, sitting up, rubbing their foreheads. Harris, motionless, watched them. His head throbbed too, as though he had been stunned by the subsonic device himself.

"Suppose you had been knocked out by the subsonic too?" Beth asked, still addressing herself to the life within the giant woman. "He would have killed us. That's what he came here for."

The subsonic could not affect me. I am beyond the reach of its powers.

Harris found his voice again. "That . . . that embryo can think and act?" His voice was a harsh, ragged whisper.

Beth nodded. "The next generation. It reaches sentience while still in the womb. By the time it's born it's fully aware, and able to defend itself while its body catches up with the abilities of its mind."

"And I thought it was a hoax," Harris said dizzily. "All this talk of a super-race. Some kind of propaganda stunt."

He felt dazed. The values of his life had been shattered in a single moment, and it would not be easy to repair them with similar speed.

"No," Beth said. "It was no hoax. No propaganda myth. And we knew you'd try to trick us when we let you go. At least, Wrynn said you would. I was naive enough to doubt him."

"Wrynn is telepathic too?"

"Yes, but only to a limited extent. He can only receive impressions. He can't transmit telepathically to others, the way his son can."

Harris frowned and said, "If you knew what I was going to do, why did you release me?"

Beth said, "Call it a test. I hoped you might change your beliefs if we let you go. I had a kind of blind faith in you. But you didn't change."

"No," Harris said. His voice was flat and lifeless. "I came here to kill you."

"We knew that the moment you stepped through the door. Wrynn detected your purpose, and his son transmitted it to us. But the seed of rebellion was in you. We hoped you might still be swayed. You failed us. You could not break away from your Darruui self."

Harris bowed his head. The signal in his body rasped again, but he ignored it.

Let Carver sweat out there, he thought. *This thing is bigger than anything Carver ever dreamed of. He can't begin to understand.*

"Tell me something," Harris said haltingly. "Don't you know what will happen to Medlin—and Darruu as well—once there are enough of these beings, once they begin to throw their weight around?"

"Nothing will happen," Beth said calmly. "None of the dire things you imagine. Do you think that they're a race of petty power-seekers, intent on establishing a galactic dominion?" The girl laughed derisively. "That sort of thinking belongs to the obsolete non-telepathic species. Us. The lower animals of the universe. These new people have different goals."

"How can you be so sure?"

"They have let us see their minds," Beth said. "We have no doubt. Power does not interest them. They have no inadequacies that they must compensate for by holding sway over others. They mean to challenge the universe itself—not the people of it."

"And we're obsolete, you say?"

"Completely."

"But these mutants wouldn't have survived if you Medlins hadn't aided them!" Harris protested. "If we're all obsolete, who's responsible? You are! You've helped your own race commit suicide—and killed Darruu in the process!"

Beth smiled oddly. "At least we were capable of seeing the new race without envy. We helped them as much as we could, because we bowed to the inevitable. We knew they would prevail anyway, given time. Their genes were too strong to be dispersed and destroyed. If we hadn't helped, it might have taken another century, perhaps, or another millennium. We preferred that they look kindly on us when they matured. Our day is done, Harris, and so is the day of Darruu, and the day of the non-telepathic Earthmans as well.''

''And ours too,'' Wrynn said mildly. ''We are the intermediates, the transitionals—the links between the old species and the new one that is emerging. I told you: my son will be as far beyond me as I am beyond my parents. You have already seen the proof of that.''

Harris nodded grimly. He felt the tension within him relax, but he did not reach for his alarm signal, for he knew that the unborn mutant could stop him with ease, moving a thousand or a million times faster than his clumsy limbs, and anticipating his decisions.

He stared at his hands—the hands of an Earthman, with Darruui flesh under the pink lining.

He thought: *all our striving is for nothing. Everything we have built is hollow.*

A new race, a glorious race, nurtured by the Medlins, brought into being on Earth. The galaxy waited for them. All of space and time lay open to them, eager for their tread. They were demigods.

He had regarded the Earthers as primitives, creatures with a mere few thousand years of history behind them, mere pale humanoids of no consequence in the galactic scheme of things.

But he had been wrong.

Long after Darruu had become a hollow world of past glories, the sons of these giant Earthers would roam the galaxies.

Looking up, he said in a choked voice, "I guess we made a tremendous mistake, we of Darruu. I was sent here to help sway the Earthers to the side of Darruu. But it's the other way around, really, isn't it? It's Darruu that will have to swear loyalty to Earth, some day soon."

"Not soon," Wrynn said. "The true race is not yet out of childhood. Twenty years more must pass before the first generation is mature. And we have enemies on Earth."

"The old Earthmen," Coburn said. "How do you think they'll like being replaced? Do you think they'll stand by with folded hands when they realize what's sprouting in their midst? They'll try to root the mutants out. They won't just nobly wave them on to inherit the future. And that's why we're here. To help the mutants until they can stand fully alone. You Darruui are just nuisances getting in the way, bringing old rivalries to a planet that isn't interested in them."

That would have been cause for hot anger, once. But now Harris merely shrugged. His whole mission had been without purpose, he saw now.

But yet, a lingering doubt remained, a last suspicion. These were Medlins. Since when were Medlins so noble, so eager to abase themselves before a new race?

The silent voice of the unborn superman said, audible to everyone in the room including Harris, *He still is not convinced, despite everything.*

"Is this so?" Beth asked.

Harris nodded. "I'm afraid the child is right," he murmured. "I see, and I hear that voice, and I believe—and yet all my conditioning tells me that it's impossible, that this could be happening. Medlins are hateful creatures; I *know* that, intuitively. And all laws of self-preservation as a race cry out against aiding mutants the way you claim to be doing."

Beth said, "Would you like a guarantee of our good faith?"

"What do you mean?"

"There is a way to show you the truth in such a way that you can have no further doubts."

"How?" Harris asked.

To the womb-bound godling Beth said, "Link us."

Nine

Before Harris had a chance to react, a strange brightness flooded over him; he seemed to be floating far above his body, and a swirl of colors danced wildly around him, a blaze of light that numbed and dazed him.

With a jolt he realized where he was.

He was looking into the mind of the Medlin who called herself Beth Baldwin. He was seeing the soul of her, laid bare. He could look through every memory of hers as clearly as though it were his own—more clearly. He could see, through her eyes, the memory of a Medlin home, of knife-bladed trees glistening bluely in the sun, of naked Medlin children splashing in a pond. Oddly, the Medlins did not look grotesque to him now. They looked—natural.

Medlin religious ceremonies came to him. Where were the human sacrifices, the blasphemous rituals he had heard about? All he saw were tame things like candle-lighting, and prayers to a Galactic Unity. The prayers sounded very much like the prayers to the Spirit, and he felt a strange sense of dislocation.

He was living Beth's life, moving along her life-line with ease, vicariously growing up with her, enduring the strains and shocks of adolescence, the tensions of a ripening body, the timidities of early love. Without embarrassment, he pried into the depths of her, since this was what she wanted him to do.

He saw none of the hideous things he had expected to find in a Medlin mind.

He saw faith and honesty, and a devotion to the truth. He saw dogged courage. He saw many things that filled him with humility.

He saw sins, but they were honest sins, honestly admitted. He saw weaknesses. He saw pettiness. She was no saint, but neither was she the demon that Medlins were held to be.

He saw her entering the service of her people, saw her training for her stint on Earth. He saw her on the operating table, surgeons bent over her to transform her into an Earthgirl. There was a dazzling glimpse of Beth in her new body, naked before a mirror, passing her hands in wonder over the soft voluptuous flesh of her new self. There was Beth learning to carry herself in a womanly way, learning to speak the Earther language idiomatically, Beth journeying to

Earth, making contact with her fellow Medlins, then with Wrynn and the other mutants.

It was a soul-searing experience, living in another's brain. He discovered what it was like to have breasts, what the emotions of a Medlin woman's ecstasies were like. He saw through her eyes how she had tracked him on his way to Earth, how she had readied herself in his hotel, how she had jostled him.

Startled, he saw himself through the filter of her mind, and the image was not a displeasing one. Her view of him was tinged with distaste for a Darruui, but there was pity as well as dislike. Why pity, he wondered, and then he saw that she pitied him simply for being a Darruui. And there were other emotions—hope, faith, even love for him, and a great abiding sorrow at the thought that he would remain forever among the enemy.

Harris trembled.

Revelation upon revelation poured through his numbed brain.

He lost touch with his own identity. He blurred, he merged, he *became* the Medlin woman who went by the name of Beth Baldwin.

And he came to pity himself.

Poor cramped bitter Darruui. Poor destroyer. Poor naysayer. Why can't you love? Why can't you embrace in open amity? Why the fear, why the envy, why the sour sullen hatred of all that's good and pure and beautiful?

That was her thought. But now it was his as well.

He thought his brain would split open from the impact of sharing his mind and hers.

All through history there have been races like yours, she was thinking. *The destroyers, the imitators, the killers of the dream. Earth has had them too: the Romans, the Assyrians, the Huns. You Darruui are of that kind.*

He shook his head doggedly. *We have culture,* he cried silently. *You simply do not know. We have religion, art, philosophy . . .*

But his own thoughts were hollow and meaningless, and he knew it. They withered and shrivelled in the bright glare of Beth's mind. His pitiful defenses of Darruui civilization could not stand up against what he now knew.

The universe rocked around him. Stars pinwheeled and burst from their orbits. And still the linkage held, still his mind was gripped tight to Beth's, still the telepathic conjugation endured. Her soul was his. Everything she had thought and hoped, feared, and loved, was his, and she was his, and he was hers, and the blast of purity and goodness was almost intolerably painful.

He could see the truth, now.

Shattering as it was, he could see it plain, and he no longer had the capacity to doubt it. The Medlins were scheming their own obsolescence. They were knowingly and eagerly working to bring the new race into being. It was a bewildering concept. It violated everything he held as rational. But they were doing it, gladly, enthusiastically, willingly.

He felt Beth's mind drawing back from his, now. Desperately, he clung to the linkage, trying to keep it intact, but he could not maintain it.

The linkage broke.

Harris stood alone, trembling, feeling as though he had been stripped naked down to the bones. He stared at Beth, a few feet from him, and he felt as though she were a part of his body that had been abruptly chopped free by the surgeon's knife.

She was smiling at him, warmly, a smile that betrayed no shame at what he might have seen in her mind.

Beth said, "Now find the mind of his leader Carver, and link him to *that*."

"No," Harris protested in horror. "Don't . . ."

It was too late.

Again the world swirled, swung, then locked into place. He sensed the smell of Darruui wine, and the prickly texture of thuuar spines, and the moons gleaming in the sky, and the plains crimson at dawn.

Then the superficial memories parted to give him a moment's insight into the deeper mind of the Darruui who wore the name of John Carver.

It was a frightening pit of foul hatreds. Harris found himself looking downward into a dark, roiling hole where writhing shapes eddied and gyred, and strange clawed creatures scrabbled hideously and waved feathery tentacles upward. Hatred, murder, every conceivable foulness was there. He could feel the cold muck oozing up out of that pit, covering him, and he shivered. There were sounds, harsh, discordant sounds, tinny cries of rage, ugly belching thunder, and beneath it all a steady sucking sound as of creatures of enormous size turning and twisting in the sticky mud. There was the occasional sharp sickening crunch of mandibles closing on breaking limbs.

It was a nightmare of unthinkable ugliness. Harris staggered backward, shivering, realizing that the Earther mutant had allowed him only a fraction of a second's entry into that mind.

He sank down onto the carpet, a miserable huddled figure, and covered his face with his hands. His mind still rocked with the vision of those nightmare things, that hideous pit of obscenities and blasphemies that churned and throbbed in the depths of John Carver's mind, beneath the outer layer of pastoral scenes of lovely Darruu.

After a moment Harris lifted his head. His mouth worked fitfully. Then he said, "What was that—those creatures?"

"Tell us what you saw," Beth said.

"I can't describe it. Animals . . . insects . . . serpents . . . everything black, shades of gray. A sickening sight, Beth. Mud and ooze and slime all over."

"The monsters of the mind," she said quietly. "The metaphors of John Carver's soul. You translated them automatically into images."

He shivered. "Are . . . we all like that?" he asked. "Every Darruui?" Am I? *Do I have those things in my mind too?*

"No," Beth said. "Not—deep down. I couldn't

have borne the linkage if you had. You've got the outer layer of hatred that every Darruui has—and every Medlin too, for that matter. But your core is good. You aren't a home for coiling monsters yet. Carver is rotten. His mind is a cesspool. It is the same with the other Darruui here.''

"I am not like that?"

"Not yet," she said.

He huddled into himself a moment more, then got uneasily to his feet. His mind was shaken as it had never been shaken before. His memory of the bond with Beth's gentle mind was overlaid by the foul horrors he had seen in Carver's mind, and his forehead throbbed with the pain of containing those two experiences.

Coburn said, "Our races have fought for centuries. A mistake on both sides that has hardened into bloodhatred. The time has come to end it."

"But how?" Harris asked. "How can we turn back and heal the gulf after so long?"

"He's right," one of the other Medlins said. "There's no way. We're too far apart now. There can't ever be a healing. We'd have to give the whole Darruui population mass psychotherapy to achieve it."

That may not be impossible, came the quiet voice of the embryo mutant.

Harris wavered at that. The thought of all Darruu being given mental therapy by these mutants—the entire world brainwashed . . .

For a moment, his old loyalties surged forward hotly, until he remembered what he had seen in

Carver's mind. *Only a sick man refuses to admit that he is sick,* Harris thought, chastened.

He said, "What can I do—to help?"

"Seek out your Darruui comrades," Beth said.

"And?"

"They must die."

Her voice was firm. Harris said, "How can you heal thousands of years of hatred with new acts of bloodshed?"

"The point is well taken," Beth said. "But we do not have time to heal your comrades. They are too far gone in hatred. They'll have to be written off. If we don't dispose of them quickly, they'll hamper us in troublesome ways we can't afford."

"You want me to kill them?"

Beth nodded silently.

Harris did not reply. He stared at nothing in particular. The five who waited for him on the street nearby were Servants of the Spirit, like himself; members of the highest caste of Darruui civilization, presumably the noblest of all creation's beings. At least, so he had been taught from the earliest.

To kill a Servant of the Spirit was to set himself apart from Darruu forever. Every man's hand would be against him. The shame of it would be impossible to conceal.

"Well?" Beth asked.

"My . . . conditioning lies deep," he said. "If I strike a blow against them, I could never return to my native planet."

"Do you *want* to return?" Beth asked.

"Of course I do!" Harris cried, surprised.

"Do you?" she asked. "Now that you've seen into the mind of a countryman? Your future lies here, don't you see that? With us."

Harris considered that. He weighed the possibility that he was still being deceived, and scowled the idea into oblivion. His suspicious Darruui nature would never rest, he saw. But it was impossible now to believe that this was Medlin deception. He had *seen*. He *knew*.

After a long moment he nodded. "Very well," he said. "Give me back the gun. I'll do the job you want."

"Once before you promised that," Beth said. "We knew then that you were lying to us."

"And now?" he asked.

She smiled and gestured to Coburn, who handed him the disruptor he had dropped. Harris grasped the butt of the weapon, hefted it, and said, "I could kill some of you now, couldn't I? It would take at least a fraction of a second to stop me. I could pull the trigger once."

"You won't," Beth said.

He stared at her. "You're right."

Ten

He rode alone in the gravshaft and emerged at street-level, in the lobby of the great building. The lobby was less crowded now. He had gone down into the Medlin headquarters in the middle of the day, but unaccountable hours had passed. It was very dark now, though the lambent glow of street-lights brightened the path. He wondered if the other five had waited for him all this time, or if they had gone along to their own places.

The stars were out in force now, bedecking the sky. Harris paused in front of the building and looked up. Up there somewhere was Darruu, not visible to the eye, but there in one of those glittering clusters all the same. Perhaps now was the time of the mating of the moons on Darruu, that time of supernal beauty that no living creature could fail to be moved by.

Well, never mind, he thought. It did not matter now.

He reached the corner where they had arranged to wait for him. Earthers moved by, rapidly, homeward bound. Harris looked around, at first seeing no one, then catching sight of Carver standing casually by the lamppost, his sharp-featured slabjawed face a study in suppressed, simmering impatience.

As Harris approached, Carver said, "You took long enough about it. Well?"

Harris stared at the other man and thought bleakly of the squirming ropy thoughts that nestled in the other's brain like festering, living snakes.

He said, "They're all dead. Didn't you get my message?"

"Sure we did. But we couldn't be sure."

"Where are the others?"

"I sent them away," Carver said. "It was too risky, hanging around here all day. How did you manage to spend so much time up there?"

"They were scattered all over," Harris said. "I was waiting to get the greatest number of them at the same time. It took time."

"Hours, though?"

"Sorry," Harris said.

He was thinking. *This man is a Servant of the Spirit, a man of Darruu. A man who thinks only of Darruu's galactic dominion, a man who hates and kills and spies, a man whose mind is a nesting-*

place for every revolting monstrosity that can be imagined.

"How many of them did you get?" Carver asked.

"Five," Harris said.

Carver looked disappointed. "Only five? After all that time?"

Harris shrugged. "The place was empty. I waited and waited, but no more showed up. At least I got five, though. Five out of a hundred. That's not bad, is it?"

"It'll do for a start," Carver said gruffly. He put his hand to his forehead and pressed it, and muttered a curse.

"Something wrong?" Harris asked.

"Headache," Carver grunted. "Hit me all at once. I feel like I've been blackjacked."

Harris looked away and smiled. "It's the gravity," he said. "It does peculiar things."

He realized that he was stalling, unwilling to do the thing he had come out here to do.

A silent voice said within him, *Will you betray us again? Or will you keep faith this time?*

The street was too busy, too crowded, even now after dark. He could not do anything here. If he activated the subsonic, people would drop like flies for forty feet around. He had to get Carver alone.

Carver was saying something to him, Harris realized. He did not hear it. Carver said again, "I asked you—were there any important documents there?"

"No," Harris said.

A cold wind swept in from the river. Harris felt a chill.

He said, "Look, let's go get a drink somewhere, Carver. I feel pretty tired out. And it'll be good for your headache too. We can celebrate—we've killed our first five Medlins."

Carver shrugged. "I wouldn't mind a drink."

They started up the street. Carver pointed to a gay, brightly-lit saloon, but Harris shook his head. "Too noisy in there. Let's find some place quiet."

They turned the corner, onto a narrow sidestreet. A winking sign at the end of the block advertised a bar, and they headed toward it. An autobar, Harris thought. That was what he wanted.

They went in.

The place was empty. Glistening banks of control devices faced them. As they crossed the threshold, a dull, booming voice from an overhead grid said, "Change is available to your left. We change any denomination of any accepted currency. Change is avail . . .

"All right!" Carver snapped. "We heard you!"

The robot voice died away. Harris took an Earther bill from his pocket and laid it across the platen of the changemaking machine. A shower of small coins came tinkling down.

"What do you recommend this time?" Harris asked.

Carver shrugged. "There's a Terran whiskey called Scotch. Very ancient. Try some."

Harris put a coin in the slot, waited, took the drink. He bought another one for Carver, and they settled down at a table. The emptiness of the bar was eerie. There were no sounds but the clicking of relays somewhere behind the facade of gadgetry, the soft purring of complex mechanisms.

Harris gulped the drink so fast he hardly tasted it. His raw, scraped nerves cried out for relaxation. He put another coin in the slot.

He watched Carver, thinking automatically of the inner world of madness that lay behind the austere, almost noble features.

He is a Servant of the Spirit, Harris thought. *He is my superior.*

It would rot the eternal roots of my birth-tree if I were to raise my hand against him.

Carver said, "I suppose it'll take us another two or three weeks to root out the rest of the Medlins. Then we'll have a free path here."

"Until more Medlins come."

"Don't worry," Carver said. "Everything's all arranged. We'll take over their headquarters and operate it as though they're still alive. Any new Medlins will be killed the moment they arrive."

Harris drained his second drink, making no comment.

Carver went on, "I've applied for augmented forces here. Word hasn't come through yet, but I'd guess that in another month we'll hear. I've asked for fifty more trained agents as a starter."

"Think you'll get them?"

"You know how it is. Ask for fifty, get twenty-five. If I asked for twenty, I'd get five. You'd think Earth wasn't important to them." Carver tapped the

empty glass in front of him and said, "Be a good
fellow and get me another drink, will you?"

"Sure," Harris said.

He slipped out from the table and walked to the
control console. That put him more than three feet
from Carver—beyond the shielding range of the subsonic. He took a deep breath, turned, and activated
the subsonic generator in his hip.

"What . . ." Carver started to say, and fell slumped
over the table, his empty glass going skittering to the
floor as his limp hand slapped it.

This was the moment, Harris thought.

His pulse raced at triple-time. His hand stole into his
pocket, his fingers closed on the small cool butt of
the disruptor. In this empty bar, with nothing but
robots around, he could squeeze off a quick shot,
finish Carver in a moment . . .

There was a clicking sound behind him. Then a
gate opened inward and some sort of mechanical
creature came rolling out from the bowels of the
autobar's mechanism.

The voice from the speaker grid overhead said, "It
violates federal law to serve intoxicating beverages to
a person who is already intoxicated. It violates federal law to serve intoxicating beverages to a person
who is already intoxicated. It violates . . ."

The mechanical creature was approaching the
slumped Carver. The robot was about three feet high,
bullet-headed and gleaming, with two telescopically
extensible arms that were sliding out of recesses in its
chest. It rolled across the floor and, as Harris gog-

gled in amazement, wrapped its arms around the unconscious Darruui, lifted him easily into the air, and continued rolling, to the door of the autobar, and out into an adjoining alleyway. A moment later, the robot returned alone.

Of course, Harris thought. An automated bouncer! Keeping watch over the patrons, making sure each drinker remained conscious, and providing a robotic bum's rush for anyone who keeled over!

The little robot vanished into its gate, which flicked shut immediately. The voice of the speaker grid died away. Gulping down his drink, Harris rushed outside, and into the alleyway.

Carver lay sprawled on the pavement. The effects of the subsonic were wearing off. He was groaning, stirring, starting to open his eyes.

This is the opportunity to destroy him, came the voice in his brain.

Harris' hand closed on the disruptor a second time. Out here, in the dark alley, a quick bolt of nerve-searing fury and it would be all over.

But he could not do it.

His entire body trembled and shook like a ghiarr-tree bending in the wind. Crisscross currents of conflicting desires rippled through him.

He closed his eyes and saw Darruu glistening in the crimson mist. Saw the annual procession of the Servants of the Spirit, each holding his candle, heard the melancholy chant, the prayer drifting back on the wind. *We are a holy fraternity. And to kill . . .*

He couldn't.

Impossible.

He hesitated, quivered, tensed. He fought with himself to bring the disruptor into aim, to squeeze the trigger, to burn the life out of the half-conscious man on the pavement.

Carver groaned.

Once again Harris saw the writhing monsters in the other's mind. Feathery limbs poked up out of the churning ooze.

Hot tears scaled Harris' eyes. He tried once more to aim the disruptor and failed. Carver stirred again.

Harris turned and fled.

Eleven

Mocking whispers followed him as he raced up the alleyway and out the other side. Coward, traitor, fool, weakling—he was all of those, and more. He told himself that he simply had not been ready. He had not come far enough, yet, to take the life of a Servant of the Spirit. Perhaps if he had had some more of the whiskey . . .

But what kind of courage was that, he asked himself, as he emerged in a brightly lit, busy street? Panicky, he ran a dozen paces, realized he was attracting attention, and slowed to a halt.

A blazing sign screamed THREE GREAT SOLLIES THREE! There was a line, disappearing into a theater. Harris joined it. He glanced fearfully over his shoulder, expecting an irate Carver to appear from the alley mouth at any moment, but no Carver appeared. The line moved slowly toward the ticketbooth. There were only five ahead of Harris now, four, three, two . . .

There was no human on duty in the booth. A gleaming change-making machine stared back at him, and a voice from a speaker grid said, "How many tickets? Half a unit apiece. How many tickets?"

Harris gaped blankly at it. The words were so much gibberish to him.

"I don't understand," he muttered, and realized that he had spoken in Darruui. Someone behind him in the line called out impatiently. A voice just behind him said, "Is there any trouble, Major?"

"I . . . I haven't been on Earth for years," Harris gasped.

"Just give the machine the money. Half a unit per ticket, that's all."

Harris found a bill in his pocket and thrust it forward. A ticket came clicking back at him. He seized it and rushed into the darkness of the theater.

"Your change, Major!" someone called from behind. But he kept going.

He found a seat. It was soft and warm and body-hugging, and he settled down into it as though crawling back into the womb. He looked up, saw the glowing screen filling a great arch in front of him and overhead, saw figures moving, heard words being uttered.

It meant nothing at all.

He sat there rigid with panic, watching the mean-

ingless three-dimensional images move about. Gradually the unreasoning blind fear receded. Words again
made sense to him. He saw that a kind of story was
being acted out. It was a meaningless story, full of
murder and brawling, and he scarcely cared what was
being shown, but imperceptibly he slipped into the
story until he was following it raptly.

His body relaxed. The tension-poisons leached out
of him as the hours passed. The first solido ended,
and a voice from the seatback in front of him let him
know that he could have refreshments in his seat by
putting coins into various slots. He ignored the
opportunity.

After a while, a second sollie began. This one was
even more inane than the first, but Harris watched it
interestedly enough, fascinated by the glowing vital-
ity of the vivid images, which seemed real enough to
touch. But as hour after hour slipped by, his calm
reasserted itself, and the rational part of his mind
became uppermost.

You certainly bungled that one, he told himself in
bitter contempt. *Carver will know you tried to kill
him, and he'll come after you. Or ambush you when
you don't expect it. You've muffed your chance.*

He expected to hear some chiding word from the
mutant telepath. But there was only silence, as there
had been since the moment in the alley when he had
been warned that this was his best chance to kill.
Since then, nothing—as though he was no longer
considered worthy of contacting.

Harris rose from his seat. Stony-faced, he walked out of the theater, into the night.

It was past midnight now. The streets were fairly quiet. He made his way carefully up the street to the helitaxi ramp.

"Spaceways Hotel," he said.

He settled back for the long trip. When he left the ramp at his destination and crossed into the hotel, he looked about warily in all directions.

The communicator signal in his body had not rasped once since he had left Carver in the alleyway. That was suspicious. Why hadn't Carver tried to contact him for an explanation, Harris wondered? Did he simply plan to close in and eliminate him without a word?

Harris sealed his room door. No one would enter without his knowledge now.

He took down his bottle of Darruui wine. It was nearly half empty, now. He had been too liberal with it the night before. Hand shaking a little, he measured out a small quantity, and sipped it as though it were the elixir of life itself.

His communicator rasped.

Tensely, he activated it. It was Carver.

"Where did you go?" Carver demanded hotly. "What happened?"

"I was frightened."

"Frightened? Is that a word for a Servant of the Spirit to use? Tell me what happened?"

"You passed out," Harris improvised. "The robot carried you to the alleyway. I thought you had been poisoned or something, that the Medlins were closing in. So I thought the best thing was for me to escape."

"And leave me there?"

"It would have done Darruu no good for both of us to be captured or killed," Harris pointed out. He was relaxing rapidly, now. Carver did not seem to suspect the real cause of his fainting spell. Unless, of course, he was simply playing a little game.

"Where are you now?" Carver asked.

"At my hotel room."

"Come to the headquarters immediately."

"At this hour?" Harris asked.

"Come to the headquarters immediately," Carver said. "Your behavior has been very strange, Major Harris. Very strange indeed."

"I've killed five Medlins tonight," Harris said. "Can't I have some rest?"

"We'll expect you within the hour," Carver said, and broke the contact.

Harris rested his head in his hands. He felt groggy. He had done too much in the past few days, covered too much ground. He simply wanted to rest . . . to rest . . .

But there was no rest for him. Wearily, he dragged himself to his feet. The thought of travelling far across the city to that weatherbeaten ancient building filled him with foreboding. There was the nagging feeling that he was going to his death, that he would perish in a dry, dusty room in some rotting building in a decayed part of the city.

He rode downstairs, shambled out the gravshaft

like a walking corpse. It seemed to him that he had spent this entire week climbing in and out of helitaxis, jaunting off to one end of the city or another. Feeling frayed and edgy, he signalled to the concierge to get him a helitaxi.

A figure came up out of nowhere and whispered softly, "You didn't succeed, did you?"

He whirled, half expecting an assassin's blow.

"Beth!"

She smiled. She had changed her clothes again, into her more seductive garb, and she was the incredibly lovely creature he had seen on his first day on Earth. He looked at her now, and his eyes met hers, and he ran through some of her memories.

Redness came to his cheeks. He was in possession of her personality, he knew the most intimate secrets of her soul. He could not bear to look her in the eye.

"The gun was in your hand," she said. "What happened then?"

"I lost my nerve. I wasn't ready."

"Perhaps we rushed you too fast."

"Perhaps."

A bellhop came up to him. "Helitaxi's waiting for you at the ramp, Major."

Harris nodded and gave the boy a coin. Beth said, "Where are you going now?"

"Out to see Carver. He's sent for me."

"Where?"

"Darruui headquarters. Way out in the slums."

"You're armed?"

"Of course."

"They're going to try to kill you, Abner. They've come to suspect your loyalty. But first they have to get you by surprise. The subsonic in your hip protects you against an attack. No one can get closer than forty feet to you against your will. So they're going to ambush you. I thought you'd like to know."

He nodded. "I figured as much."

"One more thing," she said. "An important thing."

"Yes?"

"We've intercepted a message. A dozen more Darruui agents are on their way to Earth. They'll be arriving in staggered waves over the next two months."

"So?"

"Our task becomes harder. We've got to catch them as they arrive—to root them out. We mustn't let them take hold here. We can make a beginning tonight, though. If you will help us."

"I'll try," he said.

She took his hand, held it for a moment, squeezed it. He gripped it tightly in return. It was no longer revolting to him to think that beneath the soft pink skin lay the pebbled rugosity of a Medlin pelt. He had seen through, to the essential core of her, and he could no longer hate her.

"Be careful," she murmured. "We're counting on you. When it's all over, come to our headquarters. We'll be waiting for you there."

"Beth . . ."

But it was too late. She had slipped away, as quickly as she had come. He felt a sudden fierce throbbing beneath his breastbone. The Medlins had not given up on him, he thought. They were not disgusted by his act of cowardice, by his failure to kill Carver when he had had the chance. They understood—Beth understood, at least—that such conversions as his did not happen in a moment, that he had to grope and feel his way toward the light in a twisting, zigzag course.

He stepped outside, and into the helitaxi. He gave the driver the address.

He sat back, and waited as the cab soared through the night.

At this hour, the neighborhood was even more deserted than ever. No one, no one at all was in sight. Harris approached the shabby building circuitously, watching constantly for an ambush. His heart raced. It was not normal to fear his own people; he was not accustomed to the idea of coming to grief at the hands of Servants of the Spirit, he thought.

There was a chittering sound in an alleyway, Harris, startled, clapped his hand to his hip, started to press down on the subsonic's activator. A small furry creature slithered out of the alleyway and glowered up at him, and made a tiny miauling sound.

Harris smiled in relief. *That was a close one for you, friend cat. Another moment and you'd have been extinguished.*

He knelt for a moment, scratched the animal's mangy fur, then kept going. The sound of his own footfalls echoed weirdly through the empty streets. Earth's moon, high overhead, glimmered brightly, its pockmarked face bizarre and subtly disgusting. Harris moved on.

Now he was only a block from the Aragon Boulevard headquarters. Still no ambush. He took one step at a time, kept his hand close to his hip, and advanced across the wide street, then into the building.

Upstairs.

The gravshaft creaked out its protest as it lifted his mass a hundred feet in ten seconds.

Tension mounted in his brain, his respiratory system, his belly. He could feel pores closing, feel sweat rolling down his synthetic skin. Pain drilled into him back of his eyeballs.

The gravshaft halted. He stepped out, ready to slam the subsonic into activation the moment anything menacing appeared. But the hall was empty. It was dark, too, but his Darruui eyes, accustomed to sight on a world where direct sunlight was a rarity, cut easily through the darkness as he headed toward the rooms occupied by the Darruui conspirators.

Just before he reached them, a figure detached itself from the shadows and called his name.

"Harris!"

It was Reynolds, the pudgy surgeon. His pale face was shiny with sweat. Harris scanned him for weapons, saw nothing in his hands.

"Hello, Reynolds." He eyed the pudgy man uncertainly. "What are you doing in the hall?"

"I came out for a drink. I hear your mission was a success."

"Five of them dead. A pity you and the others couldn't wait around."

"A pity," Reynolds said. "Well, if you'll step inside with me, we'll get that subsonic out of your leg—"

"Oh, you're going to remove it?"

"Of course. You don't want to walk around with a thing like that in you, do you?"

"Why not?"

"It's dangerous. It can get activated so easily. Someone jostles against you . . ."

"I'm shielded," Harris said. "If it's all right, I think I'll keep it. It's a handy little gadget. I don't understand why all agents aren't equipped with them right from the start."

Reynolds looked at him perplexedly. "You won't let me remove it?"

"I'm afraid not."

The fat man's soft lips moved soundlessly for an instant. Then, panicking, Reynolds turned and dashed through the doorway, slamming it behind him.

Harris hesitated, not caring to follow on into a possible cul-de-sac. He smiled at Reynolds' fear. The ruse hadn't worked, and Reynolds had been smitten with sudden terror. *A Servant of the Spirit.* Harris thought derisively. *The noblest creature of the universe.*

"Harris?"

It was Carver's voice, sounding hollow and indistinct from behind the closed door.

"Harris, do you hear me?"

"I hear you. What is it? Why don't you let me in, Carver?"

"Reynolds says you refuse to let him remove the subsonic."

"That's right."

"Subsonics are not part of an agent's standard equipment. It was installed on you for a specific purpose that has now been fulfilled. It must be removed at once, do you understand?"

"The Medlins aren't all dead yet," Harris said. "Five out of a hundred . . ."

"The subsonic must be removed. That's an order. Harris . . . Aar Khiilom! If you defy that order you are defying the Spirit Itself."

"All right," Harris said in a light, mocking voice. "Send Reynolds out here with his tools and he can remove the subsonic."

There was a long pause. Harris fancied he could hear whispering behind the door. No doubt the five of them were barricaded beyond the forty-foot range of the subsonic, and Reynolds was now refusing to go within its reach. The argument continued for a moment more, and at one point Harris heard Carver's voice spitting angry curses.

Then Carver called out, "Remove the subsonic yourself. We can't risk a man."

"I'm no surgeon."

"All you have to do is open the thigh-plate and detach the subsonic. Reynolds can finish the job once you've done that much."

"Sorry, but the answer is no, Carver."

"You will not defy the Spirit!"

"I will not commit suicide," Harris retorted. He knew what would happen once he had the subsonic detached. They'd fry his brains with their disruptors ten seconds later.

"I order you!" Carver thundered.

"I can't obey that order," Harris replied. "And now I'm coming in. We can finish this conversation face to face."

"Stay out. We are armed!"

"I imagine you are," Harris said.

He started for the door. They had disruptors, he knew, but the range of a disruptor was only twenty to twenty-five feet. He could reach them and stun them before they could get to him. Probably they had stunguns as well, but those lost most of their impact after a dozen yards.

He threw open the door.

He caught sight of the five of them, madly scrambling backward into one of the inner offices. He started for them, but a moment later there was a burst of flame and a splash of molten metal against the doorframe inches from his head.

Projectile guns!

Bullets!

It seemed laughable, in a way. To fall back on crude projectiles in a crisis was a pathetic way of doing business. But yet he had to admit that bullets had their advantage. They could travel great distances without losing force. They could do great damage, too.

He dropped to the floor as a second bullet thudded into the wall above him. Sighting along the floor, he measured the distance. This room was a good thirty feet long. They were in the room beyond it, which was even bigger. They had plenty of room to move around in before he would be in range. And, if they had bullet guns, they could pick him off before he could succeed in stunning them with the subsonic.

He edged forward, slithering along the floor. Another explosion sounded, another bullet slashed through the air and buried itself in the floor near him, tunnelling deep and picking up a cloud of splinters.

"This is blasphemy, Harris!" Carver called. "I order you to stop."

Harris bit down on his lip. One wild charge, he thought. That would do the trick. If he could avoid getting shot as he raced toward them . . .

"I order you in the name of the Spirit, Harris! By all you hold holy! Get away from us! Remove that subsonic! Aar Khiilom, you are destroying your own soul! You are withering the roots of your birth-tree! Do you hear me, Aar Khiilom!"

"I hear you," Harris answered.

"Obey us!"

"I can't," he replied evenly. He paused a moment, gathering strength.

Then he scrambled to his feet and rushed forward in a blind, mad dash.

Twelve

He expected to get a bullet in the face at every step. Two more shots crashed out, both of them going wild, as he raced toward the other room. He could see the five of them, now, huddled behind desks as though that could shield them from the subsonic. Patterson was the man with the gun. As Harris reached the threshold of the room, Patterson stood up and squeezed off a shot.

And scored a hit.

The bullet ripped into Harris' shoulder an inch from the cradle of bone that supported his head. He felt a shattering pain, felt bone splitting, and his head lurched wildly to the side. His left arm dangled limply, and pulsing waves of pain radiated through him. He stumbled, nearly fell.

Patterson was taking aim again.

Harris dropped to his knees. He scrabbled forward across the floor.

Reaching across his body in an awkward way, he jabbed down on the neural nexus at his hip, and activated the subsonic. In the same moment, Patterson fired, but he was falling and losing consciousness as he fell, and the shot went completely wild, flying off to the left and embedding itself in the walls.

Harris jammed hard and tingled with the kickback of the subsonic waves, and watched them fall.

Patterson, Reynolds, Tompkins, McDermott, Carver. They slipped to the floor and lay there in huddled heaps. Harris got to his feet, slowly and in great pain. He looked down at himself, saw the blood seeping its way through his torn tunic, saw the gobbets of flesh and the lances of shattered bone. If the bullet had been three inches further to the right, it would have split his chest open and ripped his heart apart.

He looked at the five unconscious men. Five Darruui wearing the skins of Earthmen. Five Servants of the Spirit.

He drew the disruptor.

It lay in his hand for a moment. Once before this evening, he had held the power of life and death over a fellow Darruui. Then it had been Carver alone, and he had been unable to fire the fatal blast. Now he had a second chance, and not only Carver but the other four as well.

He waited. He wanted a word of encouragement

from the unseen, unborn mutant whom he knew was monitoring his actions. But no word came.

He was completely on his own now.

The pain half-blinded him. He looked down at the disruptor, so tiny, so deadly. Thoughtfully he released the safety guard, pointed the snout of the instrument at Carver, took a deep breath, and squeezed the trigger. A bolt of bluish energy flared out, bathing Carver. The man gave a convulsive quiver and was still.

It was a great deal easier than he had thought.

He turned to Reynolds next, aimed the disruptor at the man's corpulent belly, squeezed.

Then Tompkins.

McDermott.

Patterson.

Five of them. Five Darruui, five Servants of the Spirit.

All dead, dead by his hand.

The pain in his shoulder suddenly became impossible to bear. He turned away from the five corpses, dropped the disruptor back in his pocket, and lurched desperately for the door. He fell on his face in five steps, and lay there, thinking that it was ridiculous not to be able to get up, absurd to lie here bleeding to death in the presence of his five victims.

But at least he had done what he had come here to do, without cowardice, without hesitation.

Well done, said the voice in his mind, breaking the silence of hours. *We were not deceived in you after all, it seems.*

Harris smiled oddly and tried to struggle to his feet. The pain was too much for him. But then the silent voice said, *You will feel no more pain*.

The throbbing died away.

Rise.

Harris fought his way to a stand.

Come forward, now. Out of there. Come to us, and we will heal you. There is more work for you to do. Other enemies to be dealt with. You have only just begun.

He staggered and lurched his way down the hall, no longer in pain but still woozy and bleeding. The nervous reaction started to swim through his body. He had killed five of his countrymen. He had come to Earth on a sacred mission, a mission of holy obligation, and he had turned worse than traitor, betraying not only Darruu but the entire future of the galaxy.

He had cast his lot with the Earthmen whose bodily guise he wore. He had joined forces with the smiling yellowhaired girl named Beth beneath whose full breasts beat a Medlin heart.

Another wave of dizziness took him as he reached the front door of the office. He paused for a moment, clung to the door, then began to walk out, slowly, in a measured tread, not looking back at the five corpses behind him.

The police would be perplexed when they held autopsies on those five, he thought, and discovered the Darruui bodies beneath the Terran flesh.

He reached the gravshaft, stepped in, flipped the

lobby indicator. Bumping sickeningly from side to side, the ancient gravshaft descended. He waited a moment in the lobby of the building, fighting back the nausea that assailed him, and then stepped outside into the clear, warm night air.

He looked up at the stars.

They spread like diamonds over the black velvet backdrop of the sky. Somewhere out there, lost in the brilliance, he knew, was Darruu. Wrapped in its crimson mist, circled by its seven moons.

He remembered the Mating of the Moons as he had last seen it: the long-awaited, mind-stunning display of beauty in the skies, and the laughter at the festival table, the singing, the hymns to the praise of the brilliance in the skies.

He knew that he would never see the Mating of the Moons again.

He could never return to Darruu now.

A strange emptiness grew in him. He felt utterly cut off, a man without a world. As he stood there, alone in the night, a helicar circled above, came to a landing in the street. A girl's head peered out.

"Abner!" Beth called. "Abner, come! Are you all right? We'll get that bullet out."

He did not reply. He took an uncertain step toward the waiting helicar, then looked up again at the stars.

The radiant sky seemed to be spurning him.

He would never return home, he told himself. He would stay here, on Earth, serving a godlike race in its uncertain infancy. He had to sever all bonds with his past. Perhaps he could manage to forget that beneath the skin of Major Abner Harris lay the body and the aching mind of Aar Khiilom, onetime Servant of the Spirit.

Forget Darruu.

Forget the fragrance of the jassaar trees and the radiance of the moons, forget the taste of the new wine, forget the kisses of the maidens.

Earth has trees that smell as sweet, it has a glorious pale moon that hangs high in the night sky, it has maidens of its own with ready lips. Put homesickness away, he ordered himself sternly.

Forget Darruu.

It would not be easy. He looked up again at the stars, trying to drink them in.

"Abner, come!" Beth called from the helicar.

He nodded distantly.

Earth was the name of his planet now, he thought. Earth.

He took a last look at the speckled sky covered with stars, and then, as he began to move toward Beth, he wondered for the last time which of the dots of brightness was Darruu. He shook his head. Darruu no longer mattered now.

Smiling, Aar Khiilom turned his face away from the stars.

Valley
Beyond
Time

One

The Valley, Sam Thornhill thought, had never looked lovelier. Drifting milky clouds hung over the two towering bare purple fangs of rock that bordered the Valley on either side and closed it off at the rear. Both suns were in the sky, the sprawling pale red one and the more distant, more intense blue; their beams mingled, casting a violet haze over tree and shrub and on the fast-flowing waters of the river that led to the barrier.

It was late in the forenoon, and all was well. Thornhill, a slim, compactly made figure in satinfab doublet and tunic, dark blue with orange trim, felt deep content. He watched the girl and the man come toward him up the winding path from the stream, wondering who they were and what they wanted with him.

149

The girl, at least, was attractive. She was dark of complexion and just short of Thornhill's own height; she wore a snug rayon blouse and a yellow knee-length lustrol sheath. Her bare shoulders were wide and sun-darkened.

The man was small, well set, hardly an inch over five feet tall. He was nearly bald; a maze of wrinkles furrowed his domed forehead. His eyes caught Thornhill's attention immediately. They were very bright, quick eyes that darted here and there in rapid glittering motions—the eyes of a predatory animal, of a lizard perhaps ready to pounce.

In the distance Thornhill caught sight of others, not all of them human. A globular Spican was visible near the stream's edge. Then Thornhill frowned for the first time; who were they, and what business had they in his Valley?

"Hello," the girl said. "My name's Marga Fallis. This is La Floquet. You just get here?"

She glanced toward the man named La Floquet and said quietly. "He hasn't come out of it yet, obviously. He must be brand-new."

"He'll wake up soon," La Floquet said. His voice was dark and sharp.

"What are you two muttering?" Thornhill demanded angrily. "How did you get here?"

"The same way you did," the girl said, "and the sooner you admit that to yourself—"

Hotly, Thornhill said, "I've always been here, damn you! This is the Valley! I've spent my whole life here! And I've never seen either of you before.

Any of you. You just appeared out of nowhere, you and this little rooster and those others down by the river, and I—'' He stopped, feeling a sudden wrenching shaft of doubt.

Of course I've always lived here, he told himself.

He began to quiver. He leaped abruptly forward, seeing in the smiling little man with the wisp of russet hair around his ears the enemy that had cast him forth from Eden. ''Damn you, it was fine till *you* got here! You had to spoil it! I'll pay you back, though.''

Thornhill sprang at the little man viciously, thinking to knock him to the ground. But to his astonishment he was the one to recoil; La Floquet remained unbudged, still smiling, still glinting birdlike at him. Thornhill sucked in a deep breath and drove forward at La Floquet a second time. This time he was efficiently caught and held; he wriggled, but though La Floquet was a good twenty years older and a foot shorter, there was surprising strength in his wiry body. Sweat burst out on Thornhill. Finally he gave ground and dropped back.

''Fighting is foolish,'' La Floquet said tranquilly. ''It accomplishes nothing. What's your name?''

''Sam Thornhill.''

''Now, attend to me. What were you doing in the moment before you first knew you were in the Valley?''

''I've always been in the Valley,'' Thornhill said stubbornly.

"Think," said the girl. "Look back. There was a time before you came to the Valley."

Thornhill turned away, looking upward at the mighty mountain peaks that hemmed them in, at the fast-flowing stream that wound between them and out toward the Barrier. A grazing beast wandered on the upreach of the foothill, nibbling the sharp-toothed grass. Had there ever been a someplace else, Thornhill wondered?

No. There had always been the Valley, and here he had lived alone and at peace until that final deceptive moment of tranquility, followed by this strange unwanted invasion.

"It usually takes several hours for the effect to wear off," the girl said. "Then you'll remember . . . the way we remember. Think. You're from Earth, aren't you?"

"Earth?" Thornhill repeated dimly.

"Green hills, spreading cities, oceans, spaceliners. Earth. No?"

"Observe the heavy tan," La Floquet pointed out. "He's from Earth, but he hasn't lived there for a while. How about Vengamon?"

"Vengamon," Thornhill declared, not questioningly this time. The strange syllables seemed to have meaning: a swollen yellow sun, broad plains, a growing city of colonists, a flourishing ore trade. "I know the word," he said.

"Was that the planet where you lived?" the girl prodded. "Vengamon?"

"I think—" Thornhill began hesitantly. His knees

felt weak. A neat pattern of life was breaking down and cascading away from him, sloughing off as if it had never been at all.

It had *never been*.

"I lived on Vengamon," he said.

"Good!" La Floquet cried. "The first fact has been elicited! Now think where you were the very moment before you came here. A spaceship, perhaps? Traveling between worlds? Think, Thornhill."

He thought. The effort was mind-wracking, but he deliberately blotted out the memories of his life in the Valley and searched backward until—

"I was a passenger on the liner *Royal Mother Helene,* bound into Vengamon from the neighboring world of Jurinalle. I . . . had been on holiday. I was returning to my—my plantation? No, not plantation. Mine. I own mining land on Vengamon. That's it, yes—mining land." The light of the double suns became oppressively warm; he felt dizzy. "I remember now: The trip was an uneventful one; I was bored and dozed off a few minutes. Then I recall seeing that I was outside the ship, somehow—and—blank. Next thing, I was here in the Valley."

"The standard pattern," La Floquet said. He gestured to the others down near the stream. "There are eight of us in all, including you. I arrived first— yesterday, I call it, though actually there's been no night. The girl came after me. Then three others. You're the third one to come today."

Thornhill blinked. "We're just being picked out of nowhere and dumped here? How is it possible?"

La Floquet shrugged. "You will be asking that question more than once before you've left the Valley. Come. Let's meet the others."

The small man turned with an imperious gesture and retraced his steps down the path; the girl followed, and Thornhill fell in line behind her. He realized he had been standing on a ledge overlooking the river, one of the foothills of the two great mountains that formed the Valley's boundaries.

The air was warm, with a faint breeze stirring through it. He felt younger than his thirty-seven years, certainly; more alive, more perceptive. He caught the fragrance of the golden blossoms that lined the riverbed and saw the light sparkle of the double sunlight scattered by the water's spray.

He thought of glancing at his watch. The hands read 14:23. That was interesting enough. The day hand said 7 July 2671. It was still the same day, then. On 7 July 2671 he had left Jurinalle for Vengamon, and he had lunched at 11:40. That meant he had probably dozed off about noon—and unless something were wrong with his watch, only two hours had passed since then. Two hours. And yet— the memories still said, though they were fading fast now—he had spent an entire life in this Valley, unmarred by intruders until a few moments before.

"This is Sam Thornhill," La Floquet suddenly said. "He's our newest arrival. He's out of Vengamon."

Thornhill eyed the others curiously. There were

five of them, three human, one humanoid, one
nonhumanoid. The nonhumanoid, globular in its
yellow-green phase just now but seeming ready to
shift to its melancholy brownish-red guise, was a
being of Spica. Tiny clawed feet peeked out from
under the great melonlike body; dark grapes atop
stalks studied Thornhill with unfathomable alien
curiosity.

The humanoid, Thornhill saw, hailed from one of
the worlds of Regulus. He was keen-eyed, pale orange in color. The heavy flap of flesh swinging from
his throat was the chief external alien characteristic
of the being. Thornhill had met his kind before.

Of the remaining three, one was a woman, small,
plain-looking, dressed in drab gray cloth garments.
There were two men: a spidery spindle-shanked sort
with mild scholarly eyes and an apologetic smile and
a powerfully built man of thirty or so, shirtless,
scowling impatiently.

"As you can see, it's quite a crew," La Floquet
remarked to Thornhill. "Vellers, did you have any
luck down by the barrier?"

The big man shook his head. "I followed the main
stream as far as I dared. But you get beyond that
grassy bend down there and come smack against that
barrier, like a wall you can't see planted in the
water." His accent was broad and heavy; he was
obviously of Earth, Thornhill thought, and not from
one of the colony worlds.

La Floquet frowned. "Did you try swimming underneath? No, of course you didn't. Eh?"

Veller's scowl grew darker. "There wasn't any percentage in it, Floquet. I dove ten–fifteen feet, and the barrier was still like glass—smooth and clean to the touch, y'know, but strong. I didn't aim to go any lower."

"All right," La Floquet said sharply. "It doesn't matter. Few of us could swim that deep, anyway." He glanced at Thornhill. "You see that this lovely Valley is likely to become our home for life, don't you?"

"There's no way out?"

The small man pointed to the gleaming radiance of the barrier, which rose in a high curving arc from the water and formed a triangular wedge closing off the lower end of the Valley. "You see that thing down there. We don't know what's at the other end, but we'd have to climb twenty thousand feet of mountain to find out. There's no way out of here."

"Do we *want* to get out?" asked the thin man in a shallow, petulant voice. "I was almost dead when I came here, La Floquet. Now I'm alive again. I don't know if I'm so anxious to leave here."

La Floquet whirled. His eyes flashed angrily as he said, "Mr. McKay, I'm delighted to hear of your recovery. But life still waits for me outside this place, lovely as the Valley is. I don't intend to rot away in here forever—not La Floquet!"

McKay shook his head slowly. "I wish there was some way of stopping you from looking for a way out. I'll die in a week if I go out of the Valley. If you escape, La Floquet, you'll be my murderer!"

"I just don't understand," Thornhill said in confusion. "If La Floquet finds a way out, what's it to you, McKay? Why don't you just stay here?"

McKay smiled unhappily. "I guess you haven't told him, then," he said to La Floquet.

"No. I didn't have a chance." La Floquet turned to Thornhill. "What this dried-up man of books is saying is that the Watcher has warned us that if one of us leaves the Valley, all the others must go."

"The Watcher?" Thornhill repeated.

"It was he who brought you here. You'll see him again. Occasionally he talks to us and tells us things. This morning he told us this: that our fates are bound together."

"And I ask you not to keep searching for the way out," McKay said dolefully. "My life depends on staying in the Valley!"

"And mine on getting out!" La Floquet blazed. He lunged forward and sent McKay sprawling to the ground in one furious gesture of contempt.

McKay turned even paler and clutched at his chest as he landed. "My heart! You shouldn't—"

Thornhill moved forward and assisted McKay to his feet. The tall, stoop-shouldered man looked dazed and shaken, but unhurt. He drew himself together and said quietly, "Two days ago a blow like that would have killed me. And now—you see?" he asked, appealing to Thornhill. "The Valley has strange properties. I don't want to leave. And he—he's condemning me to die!"

"Don't worry so over it," La Floquet said lightly.

"You may get your wish. You may spend all your days here among the poppies."

Thornhill turned and looked up the mountainside toward the top. The mountain peak loomed, snow-flecked, shrouded by clinging frosty clouds; the climb would be a giant's task. And how would they know until they had climbed it whether merely another impassable barrier lay beyond the mountain's crest?

"We seem to be stuck here for a while," Thornhill said. "But it could be worse. This looks like a pleasant place to live."

"It is," La Floquet said. "If you like pleasant places. They bore me. But come: Tell us something of yourself. Half an hour ago you had no past; has it come back to you yet?"

Thornhill nodded slowly. "I was born on Earth. Studied to be a mining engineer. I did fairly well at it, and when they opened up Vengamon, I moved out there and bought a chunk of land while the prices were low. It turned out to be a good buy. I opened a mine four years ago. I'm not married. I'm a wealthy man, as wealth is figured on Vengamon. And that's the whole story, except that I was returning home from a vacation when I was snatched off my space-ship and deposited here."

He took a deep breath, drawing the warm, moist air into his lungs. For the moment he sided with McKay; he was in no hurry to leave the Valley. But he could see that La Floquet, that energetic, driving little man, was bound to have his way. If there was any path leading out of the Valley, La Floquet would find it.

His eyes came to rest on Marga Fallis. The girl was handsome, no doubt about it. Yes, he could stay here a while longer under these double suns, breathing deep and living free from responsibility for the first time in his life. But they were supposed to be bound together: Once one left the Valley, all would. And La Floquet was determined to leave.

A shadow dimmed the purple light.

"What's that?" Thornhill said. "An eclipse?"

"The Watcher," McKay said softly. "He's back. And it wouldn't surprise me if he's brought the ninth member of our little band."

Thornhill stared as a soft blackness descended over the land, the suns still visible behind it but only as tiny dots of far-off radiance. It was as if a fluffy dark cloak had enfolded them. But it was more than a cloak—much more. He sensed a *presence* among them, watchful, curious, as eager for their welfare as a brooding hen. The alien darkness wrapped itself over the entire Valley.

This is the last of your company, said a soundless voice that seemed to echo from the mountain walls. The sky began to brighten. Suddenly as it had come, the darkness was gone, and Thornhill once again felt alone.

"The Watcher had little to say this time," McKay commented as the light returned.

"Look!" Marga cried.

Thornhill followed the direction of her pointing

arm and looked upward toward the ledge on which he
had first become aware of the Valley around him.

A tiny figure was wandering in confused circles up
there. At this distance it was impossible to tell much
about the newcomer. Thornhill became chilled. The
shadow of the Watcher had come and gone, leaving
behind yet another captive for the Valley.

Two

Thornhill narrowed his eyes as he looked toward the ledge. "We ought to go get him," he said.

La Floquet shook his head. "We have time. It takes an hour or two for the newcomers to lose that strange illusion of being alone here; you remember what it's like."

"I do," Thornhill agreed. "It's as if you've lived all your life in paradise . . . until gradually it wears off and you see others around you—as I saw you and Marga coming up the path toward me." He walked a few paces away from them and lowered himself to a moss-covered boulder. A small, wiry, catlike creature with wide cupped ears emerged from behind it and rubbed up against him; he fondled it idly as if it were his pet.

161

La Floquet shaded his eyes from the sunlight. "Can you see what he's like, that one up there?"

"No, not at this distance," Thornhill said.

"Too bad you can't. You'd be interested. We've added another alien to our gallery, I fear."

Thornhill leaned forward anxiously. "From where?"

"Aldebaran," La Floquet said.

Thornhill winced. The humanoid aliens of Aldebaran were the coldest of races, fierce, savage beings who hid festering evil behind masks of outward urbanity. Some of the out-worlds referred to the Aldebaranians as devils, and they were not so far wrong. To have one here, a devil in paradise, so to speak—

"What are we going to do?" Thornhill asked.

La Floquet shrugged. "The Watcher has put the creature here, and the Watcher has his own purposes. We'll simply have to accept what comes."

Thornhill rose and paced urgently up and down. The silent, small, mousy woman and McKay had drawn off to one side; the Spican was peering at his own plump image in the swirling waters, and the Regulan, not interested in the proceedings, stared aloofly toward the leftward mountain. The girl Marga and La Floquet remained near Thornhill.

"All right," Thornhill said finally. "Give the Aldebaranian some time to come to his senses. Meanwhile, let's forget about him and worry about ourselves. La Floquet, what do you know about this Valley?"

The small man smiled blandly. "Not very much. I know we're on a world with Earth-norm gravity and a double sun system. How many red-and-blue double suns do you know of, Thornhill?"

He shrugged. "I'm no astronomer."

"I am . . . was . . ." Marga said. "There are hundreds of such systems. We could be anywhere in the galaxy."

"Can't you tell from the constellations at night?" Thornhill asked.

"There *are* no constellations," La Floquet said sadly. "The damnable part is that there's always at least one of the suns in the sky. This planet has no night. We see no stars. But our location is unimportant." The fiery little man chuckled. "McKay will triumph. We'll never leave the Valley. How could we contact anyone, even if we were to cross the mountains? We cannot."

A sudden crackle of thunder caught Thornhill's attention. A great rolling boom reverberated from the sides of the mountains, dying away slowly.

"Listen," he said.

"A storm," said La Floquet. "Outside the confines of our barrier. The same happened yesterday at this time. It storms . . . but not in here. We live in an enchanted Valley where the sun always shines and life is gentle." A bitter grimace twisted his thin, bloodless lips. "Gentle!"

"Get used to it," Thornhill said. "We may be here a long time."

His watch read 16:42 when they finally went up the hill to get the Aldebaranian. In the two hours he had seen a shift in the configuration of the suns—the red had receded, the blue grown more intense—but it was obvious that there would be no night, that light would enter the Valley around the clock. In time he would grow used to that. He was adaptable.

Nine people, plucked from as many different worlds and cast within the space of twenty-four hours into this timeless valley beyond the storms, where there was no darkness. Of the nine, six were human, three were alien. Of the six, four were men, two were women.

Thornhill wondered about his companions. He knew so little about them yet. Vellers, the strong man, was from Earth; Thornhill knew nothing more of him. McKay and the mousy women were ciphers. Thornhill cared little about them. Neither the Regulan nor the Spican had uttered a word yet—if they could speak the Terran tongues at all. As for Marga, she was an astronomer and was lovely, but he knew nothing else. La Floquet was an interesting one—a little dynamo, shrewd and energetic but close-mouthed about his own past.

There they were. Nine pastless people. The present was as much of a mystery to them as the future.

By the time they reached the mountain ledge, Thornhill and La Floquet and the girl, the Aldebaranian had seen them and was glaring coldly at them. The storm had subsided in the land outside the Valley, and once again white clouds drifted in over the barrier.

Like all his race the Aldebaranian, a man of medium height and amiable appearance, was well fleshed, with pouches of fat swelling beneath his chin and under his ears. He was gray of skin and dark of eye, with gleaming little hooked incisors that glinted terrifyingly when he smiled. He had extra joints in his limbs as well.

"At last some others join me," the alien remarked in flawless Terran Standard as they approached. "I knew life could hardly go on here as it had."

"You're mistaken," La Floquet said. "It's a delusion common to new arrivals. You haven't lived here all your life, you know. Not really."

The Aldebaranian smiled. "This surprises me. But explain, if you will."

La Floquet explained. In a frighteningly short space of time the alien had grasped the essential nature of the Valley and his position in it. Thornhill watched coldly; the speed with which the Aldebaranian cast off delusion and accepted reality was disturbing.

They returned to the group at the river's edge. By now Thornhill was beginning to feel hungry; he had been in the Valley more than four hours. "What do we do about food?" he asked.

La Floquet said, "It falls from the skies three times a day. Manna, you know. The Watcher takes fine care of us. You got here around the time of the afternoon fall, but you were up there in your haze while we ate. It's almost time for the third fall of the day now."

The red sun had faded considerably now, and a haunted blue twilight reigned. Thornhill knew enough about solar mechanics to be aware that the big red sun was nearly dead; its feeble bulk gave little light. Fierce radiation came from the blue sun, but distance afforded protection. How this unlikely pair had come together was a matter for conjecture—some star capture in eons past, no doubt.

White flakes drifted slowly downward. As they came, Thornhill saw the Spican hoist its bulk hastily from the ground, saw the Regulan running eagerly toward the drifting flakes. McKay stirred; Vellers, the big man, tugged himself to his feet. Only Thornhill and the Aldebaranian looked at all doubtful.

"Suppertime," La Floquet said cheerfully. He punctuated the statement by snapping a gob of the floating substance from the air with a quick, sharp gesture and cramming it into his mouth.

The others, Thornhill saw, were likewise catching the food before it touched ground. The animals of the Valley were appearing—the fat, lazy-looking ruminants, the whippetlike dogs, the catlike creatures —and busily were devouring the manna from the ground.

Thornhill shrugged and shagged a mass as it hung before him in the air. After a tentative sniff he hesitantly swallowed a mouthful.

It was like chewing cloud stuff—except that this cloud had a tangy, winelike taste; his stomach felt soothed almost immediately. He wondered how such unsubstantial stuff could possibly be nourishing. Then he stopped wondering and helped himself to a second portion, then a third.

The fall stopped finally, and by then Thornhill was

sated. He lay outstretched on the ground, legs thrust out, head propped up against a boulder.

Opposite him was McKay. The thin, pale man was smiling. "I haven't eaten this way in years," he said. "Haven't had much of an appetite. But now—"

"Where are you from?" Thornhill asked, interrupting.

"Earth, originally. Then to Mars when my heart began acting up. They thought the low gravity would help me, and of course it did. I'm a professor of medieval Terran history. That is, I *was*—I was on a medical leave until—until I came here." He smiled complacently. "I feel reborn here, you know? If only I had some books—"

"Shut up," growled Vellers. "You'd stay here forever, wouldn't you, now?"

The big man lay near the water's edge staring moodily out over the river.

"Of course I would," snapped McKay testily. "And Miss Hardin, too, I'd wager."

"If we could leave the two of you here together, I'm sure you'd be very happy," came the voice of La Floquet. "But we can't do that. Either all of us stay, or all of us get out of here."

The argument appeared likely to last all night. Thornhill looked away. The three aliens seemed to be as far from each other as possible, the Spican lying in a horizontal position looking like a great inflated balloon that had somehow come to rest, the little Regulan brooding in the distance and fingering its heavy dewlap, the Aldebaranian sitting quietly to one

side listening to every word, smiling like a pudgy
Buddha.

Thornhill rose. He bent over Marga Fallis and
said, "Would you care to take a walk with me."

She hesitated just a moment. "I'd love to," she said.

They stood at the edge of the water watching the
swift stream, watching golden fish flutter past with
solemnly gaping mouths. After a while they walked
on upstream, back toward the rise in the ground that
led to the hills, which in turn rose into the two
mighty peaks.

Thornhill said, "That La Floquet. He's a funny
one, isn't he? Like a little gamecock, always jumping
around and ready for a fight."

"He's very dynamic," Marga agreed quietly.

"You and he were the first ones here, weren't
you? It must have been strange, just the two of you
in this little Eden, until the third one showed up."
Thornhill wondered why he was probing after these
things. Jealousy, perhaps? Not *perhaps*. Certainly.

"We really had very little time alone together.
McKay came right after me, and then the Spican.
The Watcher was very busy collecting."

"Collecting," Thornhill repeated. "That's all we
are. Just specimens collected and put here in this
Valley like little lizards in a terrarium. And this
Watcher—some strange alien being, I guess." He
looked up at the starless sky, still bright with day.
"There's no telling what's in the stars. Five hundred
years of space travel, and we haven't seen it all."

Marga smiled. She took his hand, and they walked on farther into the low-lying shrubbery, saying nothing. Thornhill finally broke the silence.

"You said you were an astronomer, Marga?"

"Not really." Her voice was low for a woman's and well modulated; he liked it. "I'm attached to the Bellatrix VII observatory, but strictly as an assistant. I've got a degree in astronomy, of course. But I'm just sort of hired help in the observatory."

"Is that where you were when—when—"

"Yes," she said. "I was in the main dome taking some plates out of the camera. I remember it was a very delicate business. A minute or two before it happened, someone called me on the main phone downstairs, and they wanted to transfer the call up to me. I told them it would have to wait; I couldn't be bothered until I'd finished with my plates. And then everything blanked out, and I guess my plates don't matter now. I wish I'd taken that call, though."

"Someone important?"

"Oh—no. Nothing like that."

Somehow Thornhill felt relieved. "What about La Floquet?" he asked. "Who is he?"

"He's sort of a big-game hunter," she said. "I met him once before when he led a party to Bellatrix VII. Imagine the odds on any two people in the universe meeting twice! He didn't recognize me, of course, but I remembered him. He's not easy to forget."

"He *is* sort of picturesque," Thornhill said.

"And you? You said you owned a mine on Vengamon."

"I do. I'm actually quite a dull person," said Thornhill. "This is the first interesting thing that's ever happened to me." He grinned wryly. "The fates caught up with me with a vengeance, though. I guess I'll never see Vengamon again now. Unless La Floquet can get us out of here, and I don't think he can."

"Does it matter? Will it pain you never to go back to Vengamon?"

"I doubt it," Thornhill said. "I can't see any urgent reason for wanting to go back. And you, and your observatory?"

"I can forget my observatory soon enough," she said.

Somehow he moved closer to her; he wished it were a little darker, perhaps even that the Watcher would choose this instant to arrive and afford a shield of privacy for him for a moment. He felt her warmth against him.

"Don't," she murmured suddenly. "Someone's coming."

She pulled away from him. Scowling, Thornhill turned and saw the stubby figure of La Floquet clambering toward them.

"I do hope I'm not interrupting any tender scenes," the little man said quietly.

"You might have been," Thornhill admitted. "But the damage is done. What's happened to bring you after us? The charm of our company?"

"Not exactly. There's trouble down there. Vellers and McKay had a fight."

"Over leaving the Valley?"

"Of course." La Floquet looked strangely disturbed. "Vellers hit him a little too hard, though. He killed him."

Marga gasped. "McKay's dead?"

"Very. I don't know what we ought to do with Vellers. I wanted you two in on it."

Hastily Thornhill and Marga followed La Floquet down the side of the hill toward the little group clumped on the beach. Even at a distance Thornhill could see the towering figure of Vellers staring down at his feet where the crumpled body of McKay lay.

They were still a hundred feet away when McKay rose suddenly to his feet and hurled himself on Vellers in a wild headlong assault.

Three

———

———————————

Thornhill froze an instant and grasped La Floquet's cold wrist.

"I thought you told me he was dead?"

"He *was*," La Floquet insisted. "I've seen dead men before. I know the face, the eyes, the slackness of the lips—Thornhill, this is impossible!"

They ran toward the beach. Vellers had been thrown back by the fury of the resurrected McKay's attack; he went tumbling over, with McKay groping for his throat in blind murderousness.

But Vellers' strength prevailed. As Thornhill approached, the big man plucked McKay off him with one huge hand, held him squirming in the air an instant, and rising to his feet, hurled McKay down against a beach boulder—with sickening impact. Vellers staggered back, muttering hoarsely to himself.

Thornhill stared down. A gash had opened along the side of McKay's head; blood oozed through the sparse graying hair, matting it. McKay's eyes, half-open, were glazed and sightless; his mouth hung agape, tongue lolling. The skin of his face was gray.

Kneeling, Thornhill touched his hand to McKay's wrist, then to the older man's lips. After a moment he looked up. "This time he's really dead," he said.

La Floquet was peering grimly at him. "Get out of the way!" he snapped suddenly, and to Thornhill's surprise he found himself being roughly grabbed by the shoulder and flung aside by the wiry game hunter.

Quickly La Floquet flung himself down on McKay's body, straddling it with his knees pressing against the limp arms, hands grasping the slender shoulders. The beach was very silent; La Floquet's rough, irregular breathing was the only sound. The little man seemed poised, tensed for a physical encounter.

The gash on McKay's scalp began to heal.

Thornhill watched as the parted flesh closed over; the bruised skin lost its angry discoloration. Within moments only the darkening stain of blood on McKay's forehead gave any indication that there had been a wound.

Then McKay's slitted eyelids closed and immediately reopened, showing bright, flashing eyes that rolled wildly. Color returned to the dead man's face. Like a riding whip suddenly turned by conjury into a serpent, McKay began to thrash frantically. But La Floquet was prepared. His muscles corded momentarily as he exerted pressure; McKay writhed but could not rise. Behind him Thornhill heard Vellers mumbling a prayer over and over again while the mousy Miss Hardin provided a conterpoint of harsh sobs; even the Regulan uttered a brief comment in his guttural, consonant-studded language.

Sweat beaded La Floquet's face, but he prevented McKay from repeating his previous wild charge. Perhaps a minute passed; then McKay relaxed visibly.

La Floquet remained cautiously astride him. "McKay? McKay, do you hear me? This is La Floquet."

"I hear you. You can get off me now; I'm all right."

La Floquet gestured to Thornhill and Vellers. "Stand near him. Be ready to grab him if he runs wild again." He eyed McKay suspiciously for a moment, then rolled to one side and jumped to his feet.

McKay remained on the ground a moment longer. Finally he hoisted himself to a kneeling position, and shaking his head as if to clear it, stood erect. He took a few hesitant, uncertain steps. Then he turned, staring squarely at the three men, and in a quiet voice said, "Tell me what happened to me."

"You and Vellers quarreled," La Floquet said. "He—knocked you unconscious. When you came to, something must have snapped inside you—you went after Vellers like a madman. He knocked you out a second time. You just regained consciousness."

"*No!*" Thornhill half-shouted in a voice he hardly

recognized as his own. "Tell him the truth, La Floquet! We can't gain anything by pretending it didn't happen."

"What truth?" McKay asked curiously.

Thornhill paused an instant. "McKay, you were dead. At least once. Probably twice, unless La Floquet was mistaken the first time. I examined you the second time—after Vellers bashed you against that rock. I'd swear you were dead. Feel the side of your head . . . where it was split open when Vellers threw you down."

McKay put a quivering hand to his head, drew it away bloody, and stared down at the rock near his foot. The rock was bloodstained, also.

"I see blood, but I don't feel any pain."

"Of course not," Thornhill said. "The wound healed almost instantaneously. And you were revived. *You came back to life, McKay!*"

McKay turned to La Floquet. "Is this thing true, what Thornhill's telling me? You were trying to hide it?"

La Floquet nodded.

A slow, strange smile appeared on McKay's pale, angular face. "It's the Valley, then! I was dead—and I rose from the dead! Vellers—La Floquet—you fools! Don't you see that we live forever here in this Valley that you're so anxious to leave? I died twice . . . and it was like being asleep. Dark, and I remember nothing. You're sure I was dead, Thornhill?"

"I'd swear to it."

"But of course you, La Floquet—you'd try to hide

this from me, wouldn't you? Well, do you still want to leave here? We can live forever in the Valley, La Floquet!''

The small man spat angrily. "Why bother? Why live here like vegetables, eternally, never to move beyond those mountains, never to see what's on the other side of the stream? I'd rather have a dozen unfettered years than ten thousand in this prison, McKay!" He scowled.

"You had to tell him," La Floquet said accusingly to Thornhill.

"What difference does it make?" Thornhill asked. "We'd have had a repetition sooner or later. We couldn't hide it from anyone." He glanced up at the arching mountains. "So the Watcher has ways of keeping us alive? No suicide, no murder . . . and no way out."

"There *is* a way out," La Floquet said stubbornly. "Over the mountain pass. I'm sure of it. Vellers and I may go to take a look at it tomorrow. Won't we, Vellers?"

The big man shrugged. "It's fine with me."

"You don't want to stay here forever, do you, Vellers?" La Floquet went on. "What good is immortality if it's the immortality of prisoners for life? We'll look at the mountain tomorrow, Vellers."

Thornhill detected a strange note in La Floquet's voice, a curiously strained facial expression, as if he were pleading with Vellers to support him, as if he were somehow afraid to approach the mountain alone.

The idea of La Floquet's being afraid of anything or anyone seemed hard to accept, but Thornhill had that definite impression.

He looked at Vellers, then at La Floquet. "We ought to discuss this a little further, I think. There are nine of us, La Floquet. McKay and Miss Hardin definitely want to remain in the Valley; Miss Fallis and I are uncertain, but in any event we'd like to stay here a while longer. That's four against two among the humans. As for the aliens—"

"I'll vote with La Floquet," said the Aldebaranian quietly. "Important business waits for me outside."

Troublemaker, Thornhill thought. "Four against three, then, with the Spican and the Regulan unheard from. And I guess they'll stay unheard from since we can't speak their languages."

"I can speak Regulan," volunteered the Aldebaranian. Without waiting for further discussion, he wheeled to face the grave dewlapped being and exchanged four or five short, crisp sentences with him. Turning again, he said, "Our friend votes to leave. This ties the score, I believe."

"Just a second," Thornhill said hotly. "How do we know that's what he said? Suppose—"

The mask of affability slipped from the alien's face. "Suppose *what?*" he asked coldly. "If you intend to put a shadow on my honor, Thornhill—" He left the sentence unfinished.

"It would be pretty pointless dueling here," Thornhill said, "unless your honor satisfies easily. You couldn't very well kill me for long. Perhaps a temporary death might soothe you, but let's let it drop. I'll take your interpreting job in good faith. We're four apiece for staying or trying to break out."

La Floquet said, "It was good of you to take this little vote, Thornhill. But it's not a voting matter. We're individuals, not a corporate entity, and I choose not to remain here so long as I can make the attempt to escape." The little man spun on his heel and stalked away from the group.

"There ought to be some way of stopping him," said McKay thickly. "If he escapes—"

Thornhill shook his head. "It's not as easy as all that. How's he going to get off the planet, even if he does pass the mountains?"

"You don't understand," McKay said. "The Watcher simply said if one of us *leaves the Valley*, all must go. And if La Floquet succeeds, it's death for me."

"Perhaps we're dead already," Marga suggested, breaking her long silence. "Suppose each of us—you in your spaceliner, me in my observatory—died at the same moment and came here. What if—"

The sky darkened in the now-familiar manner that signaled the approach of the Watcher.

"Ask him," Thornhill said. "He'll tell you all about it."

The black cloud descended.

You are not dead, came the voiceless answer to the unspoken question. *Though some of you will die if the barrier be passed.*

Again Thornhill felt chilled by the presence of the formless being. "Who are you?" he shouted. "What do you want with us?"

I am the Watcher.

"And what do you want with us?" Thornhill repeated.

I am the Watcher, came the inflexible answer. Fibrils of the cloud began to trickle away in many directions; within moments the sky was clear. Thornhill slumped back against a rock and looked at Marga.

"He comes and he goes, feeds us, keeps us from killing ourselves or each other. It's like a zoo, Marga! And we're the chief exhibits!"

La Floquet and Vellers came stumping toward them. "Are you satisfied with the answers to your questions?" La Floquet demanded. "Do you still want to spend the rest of your days here?"

Thornhill smiled. "Go ahead, La Floquet. Go climb the mountain. I'm changing my vote. It's five-three in favor of leaving."

"I thought you were with me," said McKay.

Thornhill ignored him. "Go on, La Floquet. You and Vellers climb that mountain. Get out of the Valley—if you can."

"Come with us," La Floquet said.

"Ah, no—I'd rather stay here. But I won't object if you go."

Fleetingly, La Floquet cast a glance at the giant tooth that blocked the Valley's exit, and it seemed to Thornhill that a shadow of fear passed over the little man's face. But La Floquet clamped his jaws tight

and through locked lips said, "Vellers, are you with
me?"

The big man shrugged amiably. "It can't hurt to
take a look, I figure."

"Let's go, then," La Floquet said firmly. He threw
one black, infuriated glance at Thornhill and struck
out for the path leading to the mountain approach.

When he was out of earshot, Marga said, "Sam,
why'd you do that?"

"I wanted to see how he'd react. I saw it."

McKay tugged at his arm fretfully. "I'll die if
we leave the Valley! Don't you see that, Mr.
Thornhill?"

Sighing, Thornhill said, "I see it. But don't worry
too much about La Floquet. He'll be back before
long."

Slowly the hours passed, and the red sun slipped
below the horizon, leaving only the distant blue sun
to provide warmth. Thornhill's wristwatch told him it
was past ten in the evening—nearly twelve hours
since the time he had boarded the spaceliner in
Jurinalle, more than four hours since his anticipated
arrival time in the main city of Vengamon. They
would have searched in vain for him by now and
would be wondering how a man could vanish so
thoroughly from a spaceship in hyperdrive.

The little group sat together at the river's edge.
The Spican had shifted fully into his brownish-red
phase and sat silently like some owl heralding the
death of the universe. The other two aliens kept

mainly to themselves as well. There was little to be said.

McKay huddled himself into a knob-kneed pile of limbs and stared up at the mountain as if hoping to see some sign of La Floquet and Vellers. Thornhill understood the expression on his face; McKay knew clearly that if La Floquet succeeded in leaving the Valley's confines, he would pay the price of his double resurrection in the same instant. McKay looked like a man seated below a thread-hung sword.

Thornhill himself stared silently at the mountain, wondering where the two men were now, how far they would get before La Floquet's cowardice forced them to turn back. He had no doubt now that La Floquet dreaded the mountain—otherwise he would have made the attempt long before instead of merely threatening it. Now he had been goaded into it by Thornhill, but would he be successful? Probably not; a brave man with one deep-lying fear often never conquered that fear. In a way Thornhill pitied little La Floquet; the gamecock would be forced to come back in humiliation, though he might delay that moment as long as he possibly could.

"You seem troubled," Marga said.

"Troubled? No, just thinking."

"About what?"

"About Vengamon, and my mine there . . . and how the vultures have probably already started to go after my estate."

"You don't miss Vengamon, do you?" she said.

He smiled and shook his head. "Not yet. That

mine was my whole life, you know. I took little vacations now and then, but I thought only of the mine and my supervisors and how lazy they were, and the price of ore in the interstellar markets. Until now. It must be some strange property of this Valley, but for the first time the mine seems terribly remote, as if it had always belonged to someone else. Or as if *it* had owned *me* and I'm free at last.''

"I know something of how you feel," Marga said. "I lived in the observatory day and night. There were always so many pictures to be taken, so many books to read, so much to do—I couldn't bear the thought of missing a day or even of stopping my work to answer the phone. But there are no stars here, and I hardly miss them."

He took her hand lightly in his. "I wonder, though— If La Floquet succeeds, if we ever do get out of this Valley and back into our ordinary lives, will we be any different? Or will I go back to double-entry bookkeeping and you to stellar luminosities?"

"We won't know until we get back," she said. "*I* we get back. But look over there."

Thornhill looked. McKay and Miss Hardin were deep in a serious conversation, and McKay had shyly taken her hand. "Love comes at last to Professor o Medieval History McKay." Thornhill grinned. "An to Miss Something-or-Other Hardin, whoever she is.'

The Regulan was asleep; the Aldebaranian stare broodingly at his feet, drawing pictures in the sand The bloated sphere that was the Spican was absorbe in its own alien thoughts. The Valley was very quiet

"I used to pity creatures in the zoos," Thornhill said. "But it's not such a bad life after all."

"So far. We don't know what the Watcher has in store for us."

A mist rolled down from the mountain peak, drifting in over the Valley. At first Thornhill thought the Watcher had returned for another visit with his captives; he saw, though, that it was merely a thin mountain mist dropping over them. It was faintly cold, and he drew Marga tighter against him.

He thought back over thirty-seven years as the mist rolled in. He had come through those thirty-seven years well enough, trim, athletic, with quick reflexes and a quicker mind. But not until this day—it was hard to believe this was still his first day in the Valley—had he fully realized life held other things besides mining and earning money.

It had taken the Valley to teach him that; would he remember the lesson if he ever returned to civilization? Might it not be better to stay here, with Marga, in eternal youth?

He frowned. Eternal youth, yes . . . but at the cost of his free will. He was nothing but a prisoner here, if a pampered one.

Suddenly he did not know what to think.

Marga's hand tightened against him. "Did you hear something? Footsteps, I think. It must be La Floquet and Vellers coming back from the mountains."

"They couldn't make it," Thornhill said, not knowing whether to feel relief or acute disappointment. He heard the sound of voices—and two figures, one small and wiry, one tall and broad, advanced toward them through the thickening mist. He turned to face them.

Four

Despite the dim illumination of twilight and the effects of the fog Thornhill had no difficulty reading the expression on La Floquet's face. It was not pleasant. The little man was angry both with himself and with Thornhill, and naked hatred was visible in his sharp features.

"Well?" Thornhill asked casually. "No go?"

"We got several thousand feet before this damned fog closed in around us. It was almost as if the Watcher sent it on purpose. We had to turn back."

"And was there any sign of a pass leading out of the Valley?"

La Floquet shrugged. "Who knows? We couldn't as much as see each other! But I'll find it. I'll go back tomorrow when both suns are in the sky—and I'll find a way out!''

"You devil," came McKay's thin, dry voice. "Won't you ever give up?"

"Not while I can still walk!" La Floquet shouted defiantly. But there was a note of mock bravado in his voice. Thornhill wondered just what had really happened up there on the mountain path.

He was not kept long in ignorance. La Floquet stalked angrily away, adopting a pose of injured arrogance, leaving Vellers standing near Thornhill. The big man looked after him and shook his head.

"The liar!"

"What's that?" Thornhill asked, half-surprised.

"There was no fog on the mountain," Vellers muttered bitterly. "He found fog when we came back down, and he took it as an excuse. The little bullfrog makes much noise, but it's hollow."

Thornhill said earnestly, "Tell me, what happened up there? If there wasn't any fog, why'd you turn back?"

"We got no more than a thousand feet up," Vellers said. "He had been leading. But then he dropped back and got very pale. He said he couldn't go on any farther."

"Why? Was he afraid of the height?"

"I don't think so," Vellers said. "I think he was afraid of getting to the top and seeing what's there. Maybe he knows there isn't any way out. Maybe he's afraid to face it. I don't know. But he made me follow him back down."

Suddenly Vellers grunted heavily, and Thornhill saw that La Floquet had come up quietly behind the big man and jabbed him sharply in the small of the back. Vellers turned. It took time for a man six feet seven to turn.

"Fool!" La Floquet barked. "Who told you these lies? Why this fairy tale, Vellers?"

"Lies? Fairy tale? Get your hands off me, La Floquet. You know damn well you funked out up there. Don't try to fast-talk your way out now."

A muscle tightened convulsively in the corner of La Floquet's slit of a mouth. His eyes flashed; he stared at Vellers as if he were some beast escaped from a cage. Suddenly La Floquet's fists flicked out, and Vellers stepped back, crying out in pain. He swung wildly at the smaller man, but La Floquet was untouchable, humming in under Vellers' guard to plant a stinging punch on the slablike jaw, darting back out again as the powerful Vellers tried to land a decisive blow. La Floquet fought like a fox at bay.

Thornhill moved uneasily forward, not wanting to get in the way of Vellers' massive fists as the giant tried vainly to hit La Floquet. Catching the eye of the Aldebaranian, Thornhill acted. He seized Vellers' arm and tugged it back while the alien similarly blocked off La Floquet.

"Enough!" Thornhill snapped. "It doesn't matter which one of you's lying. Fighting's foolish—you told me that yourself earlier today, La Floquet."

Vellers dropped back sullenly, keeping one eye on La Floquet. The small man smiled. "Honor must be defended, Thornhill, Vellers was spreading lies about me.''

''A coward and a liar, too,'' Vellers said darkly.

''Quiet, both of you,'' Thornhill told them. ''Look up there!''

He pointed.

A gathering cloud hung low over them. The Watcher was drawing near—had been, unnoticed, all during the raging quarrel. Thornhill looked up, waiting, trying to discern some living form within the amorphous blackness that descended on them. It was impossible. He saw only spreading clouds of night hiding the dim sunlight.

He felt the ground rocking gently, quivering in a barely perceptible manner. What now, he wondered, peering at the enfolding darkness. A sound like a faroff musical chord echoed in his ears—a subsonic vibration, perhaps, making him giddy, soothing him, calming him the way gentle stroking might soothe a cat.

Peace among you, my pets, the voiceless voice said softly, almost crooningly. *You quarrel too much. Let there be peace. . . .*

The subsonic note washed up over him, bathed him, cleansed him of hatred and anger. He stood there smiling, not knowing why he smiled, feeling only peace and calmness.

The cloud began to lift; the Watcher was departing. The unheard note diminished in intensity, and the motion of the ground subsided. The Valley was at rest, in perfect harmony. The last faint murmur of the note died away.

For a long while no one spoke. Thornhill looked around, seeing an uncharacteristic blandness loosen the tight set of La Floquet's jaws, seeing Vellers' heavy-featured, angry face begin to smile. He himself felt no desire to quarrel with anyone.

But deep in his mind the words of the Watcher echoed and thrust at him: *Peace among you, my pets.*

Pets.

Not even specimens in a zoo, Thornhill thought with increasing bitterness as the tranquility induced by the subsonic began to leave him. Pets. Pampered pets.

He realized he was trembling. It had seemed so attractive, this life in the Valley. He tried to cry out, to shout his rage at the bare purple mountains that hemmed them in, but the subsonic had done its work well. He could not even vocalize his anger.

Thornhill looked away, trying to drive the Watcher's soothing words from his mind.

In the days that followed they began to grow younger. McKay, the oldest, was the first to show any effects of the rejuvenation. It was on the fourth day in the Valley—days being measured, for lack of other means, by the risings of the red sun. The nine of them had settled into a semblance of a normal way of life by that time. Since the time when the Watcher had found it necessary to calm them, there had been no outbreaks of bitterness among them; instead, each went about his daily life quietly, almost sullenly, under the numbing burden of the knowledge of their status as *pets*.

They found they had little need for sleep or food; the manna sufficed to nourish them, and as for sleep, that could be in brief cat naps when the occasion demanded. They spent much of their time telling each other of their past lives, hiking through the Valley, swimming in the river. Thornhill was beginning to get terribly bored with this kind of existence.

McKay had been staring into the swiftly running current when he first noticed it. He emitted a short, sharp cry; Thornhill, thinking something was wrong, ran hurriedly toward him.

"What happened?"

McKay hardly seemed in difficulties. He was staring intently at his reflection in the water. "What color is my hair, Sam?"

"Why, gray—and—and a little touch of brown!"

McKay nodded. "Exactly. I haven't had brown in my hair in twenty years!"

By this time most of the others had gathered. McKay indicated his hair and said, "I'm growing younger. I feel it all over. And look—look at La Floquet's scalp!"

In surprise the little man clapped one hand to the top of his skull—and drew the hand away again, thunderstruck. "I'm growing hair again," he said softly, fingering the gentle fuzz that had appeared on his tanned, sun-freckled scalp. There was a curious look of incredulity on his wrinkled brown face. "That's impossible!"

"It's also impossible for a man to rise from the dead," Thornhill pointed out. "The Watcher is taking very good care of us."

He looked at all of them—at McKay and La Floquet, at Vellers, at Marga, at Lona Hardin, at the aliens. Yes, they had all changed. They looked healthier, younger, more vigorous.

He had felt the change in himself from the start. The Valley, he thought. Was this the Watcher's doing or simply some marvelous property of the area?

Suppose the latter, he thought. Suppose through some charm of the Valley they were growing ever younger. Would it stop? Would the process level off?

Or, he wondered, had the Watcher brought them all here solely for the interesting spectacle of observing nine adult beings retrogressing rapidly into childhood?

That "night"—they called the time when the red sun left the sky "night" even though there was no darkness—Thornhill learned three significant things.

He learned he loved Marga Fallis, and she him.

He learned that their love could have no possible consummation within the Valley.

And he learned that La Floquet, whatever had happened to him on the mountain peak, had not yet forgotten how to fight.

Thornhill had asked Marga to walk with him into the secluded wooded area high on the mountain path where they could have some privacy. She seemed oddly reluctant to accept, which surprised and dismayed him, for at all other times since the beginning she had gladly accepted any offers of his company. He urged her again, and finally she agreed.

They walked silently for a while. Gentle-eyed cat creatures peered at them from behind shrubs, and the air was moist and warm. Peaceful white clouds drifted high above them.

Thornhill said, "Why didn't you want to come with me, Marga?"

"I'd rather not talk about it," she said.

He shied a stone into the underbrush. "Four days, and you're keeping secrets from me already?" He started to chuckle; then, seeing her expression, he cut short his laughter. "What's wrong?"

"Is there any reason why I *shouldn't* keep secrets from you?" she asked. "I mean, is there some sort of agreement between us?"

He hesitated. "Of course not. But I thought—"

She smiled, reassuring him. "I thought, too. But I might as well be frank. This afternoon La Floquet asked me to be his woman."

Stunned, Thornhill stammered, "He—why—"

"He figures he's penned in here for life," Marga said. "And he's not interested in Lona. That leaves me, it seems. La Floquet doesn't like to go without women for long."

Thornhill moistened his lips but said nothing.

Marga went on. "He told me point blank I wasn't to go into the hills with you anymore. That if I did, he'd make trouble. He wasn't going to take no for an answer, he told me."

"And what answer did you give—if I can ask?"

She smiled warmly; blue highlights danced in her

dark eyes as she said, "Well—I'm here, aren't I? Isn't that a good enough answer to him?"

Relief swept over Thornhill like an unchecked tide. He had known of La Floquet's rivalry from the start, but this was the first time the little man had ever made any open overtures toward Marga. And if those overtures had been refused—

"La Floquet's interesting," she said as they stopped to enter a sheltered, sweet-smelling bower of thickly entwined shrubs. They had discovered it the night before. "But I wouldn't want to be number four hundred eighty-six on his string. He's a galaxy roamer; I've never fallen for that type. And I feel certain he'd never have been interested in me except as something to amuse him while he was penned up in this Valley."

She was very close to him, and in the bower not even the light of the blue star shone very brightly. *I love her*, he thought suddenly to himself, and an instant later he found his voice saying out loud, "I love you, Marga. Maybe it took a miracle to put us both in this Valley, but . . ."

"I know what you mean. And I love you, too. I told La Floquet that."

He felt an irrational surge of triumph. "What did he say?"

"Not much. He said he'd kill you if he could find some way to do it in the Valley. But I think that'll wear off soon."

His arm slipped around hers. They spoke wordlessly with one another for several moments.

It was then that Thornhill discovered that sex was

impossible in the Valley. He felt no desire, no tingling of need, *nothing*.

Absolutely nothing. He enjoyed her nearness, but neither needed nor could take anything more.

"It's part of the Valley," he whispered. "Our entire metabolic systems have been changed. We don't sleep more than an hour a day, we hardly eat (unless you call that fluff food), our wounds heal, the dead rise—and now this. It's as if the Valley casts a spell that short-circuits all biological processes."

"And there's nothing we can do?"

"Nothing," he said tightly. "We're pets. Growing ever younger and helpless against the Watcher's whims."

He stared silently into the darkness, listening to her quiet sobbing. How long can we go on living this way, he wondered. How long?

We have to get out of this Valley, he thought. *Somehow.*

But will we remember one another once we do? Or will it all fade away like a child's dream of fairyland?

He clung tightly to her, cursing his own weakness even though he knew it was hardly his fault. There was nothing they could say to one another.

But the silence was abruptly broken.

A deep, dry voice said, "I know you're in there. Come on out, Thornhill. And bring the girl with you."

Thornhill quickly rose to a sitting position. "It's La Floquet!" he whispered.

"What are you going to do? Can he find us in here?"

"I'm sure of it. I'm going to have to go out there and see what he wants."

"Be careful, Sam!"

"He can't hurt me. This is the Valley, remember?" He grinned at her and clambered to his feet, stooping as he passed through the clustered underbrush. He blinked as he made the transition from darkness to pale light.

"Come on out of there, Thornhill!" La Floquet repeated. "I'll give you another minute, and then I'm coming in!"

"Don't fret," Thornhill called. "I'm on my way out."

He battled past two clinging, enwrapped vines and stepped into the open. "Well, what do you want?" he demanded impatiently.

La Floquet smiled coldly. There was little doubt of what he wanted. His small eyes were bright with anger, and there was murder in his grin. Held tight in one lean, corded hand was a long, triangular sliver of rock whose jagged edge had been painstakingly abraded until it was knife-sharp. The little man waited in a half-crouch, like a tiger or a panther impatient to spring on its prey.

Five

They circled tentatively around each other, the big man and the small one. La Floquet seemed to have reached a murderous pitch of intensity; muscles quivered in his jaws as he glared at Thornhill.

"Put that knife down," Thornhill said. "Have you blown your stack, La Floquet? You can't kill a man in the Valley. It won't work."

"Perhaps I can't kill a man. Still, I can wound him."

"What have I ever done to you?"

"You came to the Valley. I could have handled the others, but you—! You were the one who taunted me into climbing the mountain. You were the one who took Marga."

"I didn't take anyone. You didn't see me twisting

196

her arm. She picked me over you, and for that I'm genuinely sorry."

"You'll be more than sorry, Thornhill!"

Thornhill forced a grin. This little kill dance had gone on too long as it was. He sensed Marga not far behind him watching in horror.

"Why you murderous little paranoid, give me that piece of stone before you slash yourself up!" He took a quick step forward, reaching for La Floquet's wrist. The little man's eyes blazed dangerously. He pirouetted backward, snapping a curse at Thornhill in some alien language, and drove the knife downward with a low cry of triumph.

Thornhill swerved, but the jagged blade ripped into his arm three inches above the elbow, biting into the soft flesh on the inside of his biceps, and La Floquet sliced quickly downward, cutting a bloody trail for nearly eight inches. Thornhill felt a sudden sharp burst of pain down to the middle of his forearm, and a warm flow of blood gushed past his wrist into the palm of his hand. He heard Marga's sharp gasp.

Then he moved forward, ignoring the pain, and caught La Floquet's arm just as the smaller man was lifting it for a second slash. Thornhill twisted; something snapped in La Floquet's arm, and the little man gave forth a brief moan of pain. The knife dropped from suddenly uncontrollable fingers and landed lightly on an angle, its tip resting on a pebble. Thornhill planted his foot on the dagger and leaned down heavily, shattering it.

Each of them now had only limited use of his right

hand. La Floquet charged back toward Thornhill like someone possessed, head down as if to butt, but at the last moment swerved upward, driving his good hand into Thornhill's jaw. Thornhill rocked backward, pivoted around, smashed down at La Floquet, and heard teeth splinter. He wondered when the Watcher would show up to end the fight—and whether these wounds would heal.

La Floquet's harsh breathing was the only sound audible. He was shaking his head, clearing it, readying himself for a new assault. Thornhill tried to blank out the searing pain of the gash in his arm.

He stepped forward and hit La Floquet quickly, spinning him half around; bringing his slashed right hand up, Thornhill drove it into La Floquet's middle. A wall of rocklike muscle stunned his fist. But the breath had been knocked from La Floquet; he weaved uncertainly, gray-faced, wobbly-legged. Thornhill hit him again, and he toppled.

La Floquet crumpled into an awkward heap on the ground and stayed there. Thornhill glanced at his own arm. The cut was deep and wide, though it seemed to have missed any major veins and arteries; blood welled brightly from it, but without the familiar arterial spurt.

There was a curious fascination in watching his own blood flow. He saw Marga's pale, frightened face beyond the dim haze that surrounded him; he realized he had lost more blood than he thought, perhaps was about to lose consciousness as well. La

Floquet still slumbered. There was no sign of the Watcher.

"Sam—"

"Pretty little nick, isn't it?" He laughed. His face felt warm.

"We ought to bind that some way. Infection—"

"No. There's no need of that. I'll be all right. This is the Valley."

He felt an intense itching in the wounded arm; barely did he fight back the desire to claw at the gash with his fingernails.

"It's—it's healing!" Marga said.

Thornhill nodded. The wound was beginning to close. First the blood ceased flowing as ruptured veins closed their gaping sides and once again began to circulate the blood. The raw edges of the wound strained toward each other, puckering, reaching for one another, finally clasping. A bridge of flesh formed over the gaping slit in his arm. The itching was impossibly intense.

But in a few moments more it was over; a long livid scar remained, nothing more. Experimentally he touched the new flesh; it was warm, yielding, real.

La Floquet was stirring. His right forearm had been bent at an awkward angle; now it straightened out. The little man sat up groggily. Thornhill tensed in case further attack was coming, but there was very little fight left in La Floquet.

"The Watcher has made the necessary repairs," Thornhill said. "We're whole again except for a scar here and there. Get up, you idiot."

He hoisted La Floquet to his feet.

"This is the first time anyone has bested me in a fight," La Floquet said bitterly. His eyes had lost much of their eager brightness; he seemed demolished by his defeat. "And you were unarmed, and I had a knife."

"Forget that," Thornhill said.

"How can I? This filthy Valley—from which there is no escape, not even suicide—and I am not to have a woman. Thornhill, you're just a businessman. You don't know what it's like to set codes of behavior for yourself and then not be able to live by them." La Floquet shook his head sadly. "There are many in the galaxy who would rejoice to see the way this Valley has humiliated me. And there is not even suicide here! But I'll leave you with your woman."

He turned and began to walk away, a small, almost pathetic figure now, the fighting cock with his comb shorn and his tail feathers plucked. Thornhill contrasted him with the ebullient little figure he had first seen coming toward him up the mountain path, and it was a sad contrast indeed. He slouched now, shoulders sloping in defeat.

"Hold it, La Floquet!"

"You have beaten me—and before a woman. What more do you want with me, Thornhill?"

"How badly do you want to get out of this Valley?" Thornhill asked bluntly.

"What—"

"Badly enough to climb that mountain again?"

La Floquet's face, pale already, turned almost

ghostly beneath his tan. In an unsteady voice he said, "I ask you not to taunt me, Thornhill."

"I'm not. I don't give a damn what phobia it is that drove you back from the mountain that night. I think that mountains can be climbed. But not by one or two men. If we *all* went up there—or most of us—"

La Floquet smiled wanly. "You would go, too? And Marga?"

"If it means out, yes. We might have to leave McKay and Lona Hardin behind, but there'd still be seven of us. Possibly there's a city outside the Valley; we might be able to send word and be rescued."

Frowning, La Floquet said, "Why the sudden change of heart, Thornhill? I thought you liked it here . . . you and Miss Fallis both, that is. I thought *I* was the only one willing to climb that peak."

Thornhill glanced at Marga and traded secret smiles with her. "I'll decline to answer that, La Floquet. But I'll tell you this: The quicker I'm outside the influence of the Valley, the happier I'll be!"

When they had reached the foot of the hill and called everyone together, Thornhill stepped forward. Sixteen eyes were on him—counting the two stalked objects of the Spican as eyes.

He said, "La Floquet and I have just had a little discussion up in the hill. We've reached a few conclusions I want to put forth to the group at large.

"I submit that it's necessary for the well-being of all of us to make an immediate attempt at getting out of the Valley. Otherwise, we're condemned to a slow death of the most horrible kind—gradual loss of our faculties.''

McKay broke in, saying, "Now you've shifted sides again, Thornhill! I thought maybe—"

"I haven't been on any side," he responded quickly. "It's simply that I've begun thinking. Look: We were all brought here within a two-day span, snatched out of our lives no matter where we were, dumped down in a seemingly impassable Valley by some unimaginably alien creature. Item: We're watched constantly, tended and fed. Item: Our wounds heal almost instantly. Item: We're growing younger. McKay, you yourself were the first to notice that.

"Okay, now. There's a mountain up there, and quite probably there's a way out of the Valley. La Floquet tried to get there, but he and Vellers couldn't make it; two men can't climb a twenty-thousand-foot peak alone without provisions, without help. But if we all go—"

McKay shook his head. "I'm happy here, Thornhill. You and La Floquet are jeopardizing that happiness."

"No," La Floquet interjected. "Can't you see that we're just house pets here? That we're the subjects of a rather interesting experiment, nothing more? And that if this rejuvenation keeps up, we may all be babies in a matter of weeks or months?"

"I don't care," McKay said stubbornly. "I'll die if I leave the Valley—my heart can't take much more. Now you tell me I'll die if I stay. But at least I'll pass backward through manhood before I go— and I can't have those years again outside."

"All right," Thornhill said. "Ultimately it's a matter of whether we all stay here so McKay can enjoy his youth again, or whether we try to leave. La Floquet, Marga, and I are going to make an attempt to cross the mountain. Those of you who want to join us can. Those of you who'd rather spend the rest of their days in the Valley can stay behind and wish us bad luck. Is that clear?"

Seven of them left the following "morning," right after the breakfast-time manna fall. McKay stayed behind with little Lona Hardin. There was a brief, awkward moment of farewell-saying. Thornhill noticed how the lines were leaving McKay's face, how the old scholar's hair had darkened, his body broadened. In a way he could see McKay's point of view, but there was no way he could accept it.

Lona Hardin, too, was younger looking, and perhaps for the first time in her life she was making an attempt to disguise her plainness. Well, Thornhill thought, these two might find happiness of a sort in the Valley, but it was the mindless happiness of a puppet, and he wanted none of it for himself.

"I don't know what to say," McKay declared as the party set out. "I'd wish you good luck—if I could."

Thornhill grinned. "Maybe we'll be seeing you two again. I hope not, though."

Thornhill led the way up the mountain's side; Marga walked with him, La Floquet and Vellers a few paces behind, the three aliens trailing behind them. The

Spican, Thornhill was sure, had only the barest notion of what was taking place; the Aldebaranian had explained things fairly thoroughly to the grave Regulan. One factor seemed common: All of them were determined to leave the Valley.

The morning was warm and pleasant; clouds hid the peak of the mountains. The ascent, Thornhill thought, would be strenuous but not impossible—provided the miraculous field of the Valley continued to protect them when they passed the timberline and provided the Watcher did not interfere with the exodus.

There was no interference. Thornhill felt almost a sensation of regret at leaving the Valley and in the same moment realized this might be some deceptive trick of the Watcher's, and he cast all sentiment from his heart.

By midmorning they had reached a considerable height, a thousand feet or more above the Valley. Looking down, Thornhill could barely see the brightness of the river winding through the flat basin that was the Valley, and there was no sign of McKay far below.

The mountain sloped gently upward toward the timberline. The real struggle would begin later, perhaps, on the bare rock face, where the air might not be so balmly as it was here, the wind not quite as gentle.

When Thornhill's watch said noon, he called a halt and they unpacked the manna—wrapped in the broad, coarse, velvet-textured leaves of the thick-trunked trees of the Valley—they had saved from the morning fall. The manna tasted dry and stale, almost like straw, with just the merest vestige of its former attractive flavor. But as Thornhill had guessed, there was no noontime manna fall here on the mountain slope, and so the party forced the dry stuff down their throats, not knowing when they would have fresh food again.

After a short rest Thornhill ordered them up. They had gone no more than a thousand feet when an echoing cry drifted up from below:

"Wait! Wait, Thornhill!"

He turned. "You hear something?" he asked Marga.

"That was McKay's voice," La Floquet said.

"Let's wait for him," Thornhill ordered.

Ten minutes passed, and then McKay came into view, running upward in a springy long-legged stride, Lona Hardin a few paces behind him. He caught up with the party and paused a moment, catching his breath.

"I decided to come along," he said finally. "You're right, Thornhill! We have to leave the Valley."

"And he figures his heart's better already," Lona Hardin said. "So if he leaves the Valley now, maybe he'll be a healthier man again."

Thornhill smiled. "It took a long time to convince you, didn't it?" He shaded his eyes and stared upward. "We have a long way to go. We'd better not waste any more time."

Six

Twenty thousand feet is less than four miles. A man should be able to walk four miles in an hour or two. But not four miles *up*.

They rested frequently, though there was no night and they had no need of sleep. They moved on inch by inch, advancing perhaps five hundred feet over the steadily more treacherous slope, then crawling along the mountain face a hundred feet to find the next point of ascent. It was slow, difficult work, and the mountain spired yet higher above them until it seemed they would never attain the summit.

The air, surprisingly, remained warm, though not oppressively so; the wind picked up as they climbed. The mountain was utterly bare of life; the gentle animals of the Valley ventured no higher than the timberline, and that was far below. The party of nine scrambled up over rock falls and past sheets of stone.

Thornhill felt himself tiring, but he knew the Valley's strange regenerative force was at work, carrying off the fatigue poisons as soon as they built up in his muscles, easing him, giving him the strength to go on. Hour after hour they forced their way up the mountainside.

Occasionally he would glance back to see La Floquet's pale, fear-tautened face. The little man was terrified of the height, but he was driving gamely on. The aliens straggled behind; Vellers marched mechanically, saying little, obviously tolerant of the weaker mortals to whose pace he was compelled to adjust his own.

As for Marga, she uttered no complaint. That pleased Thornhill more than anything.

They were a good thousand feet from the summit when Thornhill called a halt.

He glanced back at them—at the oddly unweary, unlined faces. *How we've grown young!* he thought suddenly. *McKay looks like a man in his late forties; I must seem like a boy. And we're all fresh as daisies, as if this were just a jolly hike.*

"We're near the top," he said. "Let's finish off whatever of the manna we've got. The downhill part of this won't be so bad."

He looked up. The mountain tapered to a fine crest, and through there a pass leading down to the other side was visible. "La Floquet, you've got the best eyes of any of us. You seen any sign of a barrier up ahead?"

The little man squinted and shook his head. "All's clear so far as I can see. We go up, then down, and we're home free."

Thornhill nodded. "The last thousand feet, then. Let's go!"

The wind was whipping hard against them as they pushed on through the dense snow that cloaked the mountain's highest point. Up here some of the charm of the Valley seemed to be gone, as if the cold winds barreling in from the outlands beyond the crest could in some way negate the gentle warmth they experienced in the Valley. Both suns were high in the sky, the red and the blue, the blue visible as a hard blotch of radiance penetrating the soft, diffuse rays of the red.

Thornhill was tiring rapidly, but the crest was in sight. Just a few more feet and they'd stand on it—

Just up over the overhang—

The summit itself was a small plateau, perhaps a hundred feet long. Thornhill was the first to pull himself up over the rock projection and stand on the peak; he reached back, helped Marga up, and within minutes the other seven had joined them.

The Valley was a distant spot of green far below; the air was clear and clean, and from here they could plainly see the winding river heading down valley to the yellow-green radiance of the barrier.

Thornhill turned. "Look down there," he said in a quiet voice.

"It's a world of deserts!" La Floquet exclaimed.

The view from the summit revealed much of the land beyond the Valley, and it seemed the Valley was but an oasis in the midst of utter desert. For mile after gray mile, barren land stretched before them, an endless plain of rock and sand rolling on drearily to the farthest horizon.

Beyond, this. Behind, the Valley.

Thornhill looked around. "We've reached the top. You see what's ahead. Do we go on?"

"Do we have any choice?" McKay asked. "We're practically out of the Watcher's hands now. Down there perhaps we have freedom. Behind us—"

"We go on," La Floquet said firmly.

"Down the back slope, then," said Thornhill. "It won't be easy. There's the path over there. Suppose we—"

The sudden chill he felt was not altogether due to the whistling wind. The sky suddenly darkened; a cloak of night settled around them.

Of course, Thornhill thought dully. *I should have foreseen this.*

"The Watcher's coming!" Lona Hardin screamed as the darkness, obscuring both the bleakness ahead and the Valley behind, closed around them.

Thornhill thought, *It was part of the game. To let us climb the mountain, to watch us squirm and struggle, and then to hurl us back into the Valley at the last moment as we stand on the border.*

Wings of night nestled around them. He felt the coldness that signified the alien presence, and the soft voice said, *Would you leave, my pets? Don't I give you the best of care? Why this ingratitude?*

"Let's keep going," Thornhill muttered. "Maybe it can't stop us. Maybe we can escape it yet."

"Which way do we go?" Marga asked. "I can't see anything. Suppose we go over the edge?"

Come, crooned the Watcher, *come back to the Valley. You have played your little game. I have enjoyed your struggles, and I'm proud of the battle you fought. But the time has come to return to the warmth and the love you may find in the Valley below—*

"Thornhill!" cried La Floquet suddenly, hoarsely. "I have it! Come help me!"

The Watcher's voice died away abruptly; the black cloud swirled wildly. Thornhill whirled, peering through the darkness for some sign of La Floquet—

And found the little man on the ground, wrestling with—something. In the darkness, it was hard to tell—

"It's the Watcher!" La Floquet grunted. He rolled over, and Thornhill saw a small snakelike being writhing under La Floquet's grip, a bright-scaled serpent the size of a monkey.

"Here in the middle of the cloud—*here's* the creature that held us here!" La Floquet cried. Suddenly, before Thornhill could move, the Aldebaranian came bounding forward, thrusting beyond Thornhill and Marga, and flung himself down on the strugglers. Thornhill heard a guttural bellow; the darkness closed in on the trio, and it was impossible to see what was happening.

He heard La Floquet's cry: "Get . . . this devil . . . off me! He's helping the Watcher!"

Thornhill moved forward. He reached into the struggling mass, felt the blubbery flesh of the Aldebaranian, and dug his fingers in hard. He wrenched; the Aldebaranian came away. Hooked claws raked Thornhill's face. He cursed; you could never tell what an Aldebaranian was likely to do at any time. Perhaps the creature had been in league with the Watcher all along.

He dodged a blow, landed a solid one in the alien's plump belly, and crashed his other fist upward into the creature's jaw. The Aldebaranian rocked backward. Vellers appeared abruptly from nowhere and seized the being.

"No!" Thornhill yelled, seeing what Vellers intended. But it was too late. The giant held the Aldebaranian contemptuously dangling in the air, then swung him upward and outward. A high ear-piercing shriek resounded. Thornhill shuddered. It takes a long time to fall twenty thousand feet.

He glanced back now at La Floquet and saw the small man struggling to stand up, arms still entwined about the serpentlike being. Thornhill saw a metal-mesh helmet on the alien's head. The means by which they'd been controlled, perhaps.

La Floquet took three staggering steps. "Get the helmet off him!" he cried thickly. "I've seen these before. They are out of the Andromeda sector . . . telepaths, teleports . . . deadly creatures. The helmet's his focus point."

Thornhill grasped for it as the pair careened by; he missed, catching instead a glimpse of the Watcher's devilish, hate-filled eyes. The Watcher had fallen into the hands of his own pets—and was not enjoying it.

"I can't see you!" Thornhill shouted. "I can't get the helmet!"

"If he gets free, we're finished," came La Floquet's voice. "He's using all his energy to fight me off . . . but all he needs to do is turn on the subsonics—"

The darkness cleared again. Thornhill gasped. La Floquet, still clutching the alien, was tottering on the edge of the mountain peak, groping for the helmet in vain. One of the little man's feet was virtually standing on air. He staggered wildly. Thornhill rushed toward them, grasped the icy metal of the helmet, and ripped it away.

In that moment both La Floquet and the Watcher vanished from sight. Thornhill brought himself up short and peered downward, hearing nothing, seeing nothing—

There was just one scream . . . not from La Floquet's throat but from the alien's. Then all was silent. Thornhill glanced at the helmet in his hands, thinking of La Floquet, and in a sudden impulsive gesture hurled the little metal headpiece into the abyss after them.

He turned, catching one last glimpse of Marga, Vellers, McKay, Lona Hardin, and the Regulan, and the Spican. Then, before he could speak, mountain peak and darkness and indeed the entire world shimmered and heaved dizzingly about them, and he could see nothing and no one.

*   *   *

He was in the main passenger cabin of the Federa-
on Spaceliner *Royal Mother Helene* bound for
'engamon out of Jurinalle. He was lying back in the
omfortable pressurized cabin, the gray nothingness
f hyperspace outside forming a sharp contrast to the
idiant walls of the cabin, which glowed in soft
ellow luminescence.

Thornhill opened his eyes slowly. He glanced at
is watch: 12:13, *7 July* 2671. He had dozed off
bout 11:40 after a good lunch. They were due in at
ort Vengamon later that day, and he would have to
nd to mine business immediately. There was no
lling how badly they had fouled things up in the
me he had been vacationing on Jurinalle.

He blinked. Of a sudden, strange images flashed
ito his eyes—a valley somewhere on a barren, deso-
ite planet beyond the edge of the galaxy. A moun-
in peak, and a strange alien being, and a brave little
ian falling to the death he dreaded, and a girl—

It couldn't have been a dream, he told himself.
*o. Not a dream. It was just that the Watcher yanked
s out of space-time for his little experiment, and
hen I destroyed the helmet, we re-entered the con-
nuum at the instant we had left it.*

A cold sweat burst out suddenly all over his body.
hat means, he thought, *that La Floquet's not dead.
nd Marga—Marga—*

Thornhill sprang from his gravity couch, ignoring
e sign that urged him to PLEASE REMAIN IN
OUR COUCH WHILE SHIP IS UNDERGOING
PIN, and rushed down the aisle toward the steward.

He gripped the man by the shoulder, spun him around.

"Yes, Mr. Thornhill? Is anything wrong? You could have signaled me, and—"

"Never mind that. I want to make a subradio call to Bellatrix VII."

"We'll be landing on Vengamon in a couple of hours, sir. Is it so urgent?"

"Yes."

The steward shrugged. "You know, of course, that shipboard subradio calls may take some time to put through, and that they're terribly expensive—"

"Damn the expense, man! Will you put through my call or won't you?"

"Of course, Mr. Thornhill. To whom?"

He paused and said carefully, "To Miss Marga Fallis, in some observatory on Bellatrix VII." He peeled a bill from his wallet and added, "Here. There'll be another one for you if the call's put through in the next half an hour. I'll wait."

The summons finally came. "Mr. Thornhill, your call's ready. Would you come to Communications Deck, please?"

They showed him to a small, dimly lit cubicle. There could be no vision on an interstellar subradio call, of course, just voice transmission. But that would be enough. "Go ahead, Bellatrix-*Helene*. The call is ready," an operator said.

Thornhill wet his lips. "Marga? This is Sam—Sam Thornhill!"

"Oh!" He could picture her face now. "It—it wasn't a dream, then. I was so afraid it was!"

"When I threw the helmet off the mountain, the Watcher's hold was broken. Did you return to the exact moment you had left?"

"Yes," she said. "Back in the observatory, with my camera plates and everything. And there was a call for me, and at first I was angry and wouldn't answer it the way I always won't answer, and then I thought a minute and had a wild idea and changed my mind—and I'm glad I did, darling!"

"It seems almost like a dream, doesn't it? The Valley, I mean. And La Floquet, and all the others. But it wasn't any dream," Thornhill said. "We were really there. And I meant the things I said to you."

The operator's voice cut in sharply: *"Standard call time has elapsed, sir. There will be an additional charge of ten credits for each further fifteen-second period of your conversation."*

"That's quite all right, Operator," Thornhill said. "Just give me the bill at the end. Marga, are you still there?"

"Of course, darling."

"When can I see you?"

"I'll come to Vengamon tomorrow. It'll take a day or so to wind things up here at the observatory. Is there an observatory on Vengamon?"

"I'll build you one," Thornhill promised. "And perhaps for our honeymoon we can go looking for the Valley."

"I don't think we'll ever find it," she said. "But

we'd better hang up now. Otherwise you'll become a pauper talking to me."

He stared at the dead phone a long moment after they broke contact, thinking of what Marga looked like, and La Floquet, and all the others. Above all, Marga.

It wasn't a dream, he told himself. He thought of the shadow-haunted Valley where night never fell and men grew younger, and of a tall girl with dark flashing eyes who waited for him now half a galaxy away.

With quivering fingers he undid the sleeve of his tunic and looked down at the long, livid scar that ran almost the length of his right arm, almost to the wrist. Somewhere in the universe now was a little man named La Floquet who had inflicted that wound and died and returned to his point of departure, who now was probably wondering if it had all ever happened. Thornhill smiled, forgiving La Floquet for the ragged scar inscribed on his arm, and headed up the companionway to the passenger cabin, impatient now to see Vengamon once more.

POUL ANDERSON
Winner of 7 Hugos and 3 Nebulas

Buy them at your local bookstore or use this handy coupon:
Clip and mail this page with your order

TOR BOOKS—Reader Service Dept.
P.O. Box 690, Rockville Centre, N.Y. 11571

Please send me the book(s) I have checked above. I am enclosing
$_____ (please add $1.00 to cover postage and handling).
Send check or money order only—no cash or C.O.D.'s.

Mr./Mrs./Miss _____

Address _____

City _____ State/Zip _____

Please allow six weeks for delivery. Prices subject to change without notice.